Girlf

D0976152

"What d'you think? Shall we go? Cos I've told them that we will, but if you'd rather not–"

"I don't mind," said Rees. "We can go if you like."

"Are you sure?" I squeaked at him, ecstatically. "I just thought it would be fun."

"Your wish is my command," said Rees.

It kills me when he says stuff like that! We arranged to meet at the station at eight-thirty on Saturday morning, and I went racing jubilantly downstairs to tell Mum. I couldn't help feeling how lucky I was, having a boyfriend like Rees. Always so polite, and so considerate. He would never do anything to upset me, or embarrass me. I said very solemnly to Mum, "When I consider how some people's boyfriends behave, I know I have cause to be grateful."

Mum seemed to find this amusing, I'm not quite sure why, but she agreed that Rees was "One in a million…you hang onto him!"

"I intend to," I said.

She laughed at that. I still don't see what was funny about it.

Also by Jean Ure
in the Girlfriends series

Girls Stick Together!

Girls Are Groovy!

Pink Knickers Aren't Cool!

Boys Are OK!

Boys R Us

Orchard Black Apples

Get a Life

Just Sixteen

Love is for Ever

ORCHARD BOOKS
338 Euston Road, London NW1 3BH
Orchard Books Australia
Level 17/207 Kent Street, Sydney, NSW 2000
First published in 2009 by Orchard Books
ISBN 978 1 40830 302 3
Text © Jean Ure 2009
The right of Jean Ure to be identified as the author of this work has been asserted
by her in accordance with the Copyright, Designs and Patents Act, 1988.
A CIP catalogue record for this book is available from the British Library.
1 3 5 7 9 10 8 6 4 2
Printed in Great Britain
Orchard Books is a division of Hachette Children's Books,
an Hachette UK company.
www.hachette.co.uk

Boys will Be Boys

JEAN URE

ORCHARD BOOKS

Chapter 1

"So who is with who?" demanded Chloe. "Tell me! I want to know."

"OK. Well, Frizz," I said, "is still with Darren—"

"*Still?*" Chloe shrieked at me. "After all this time? I can't believe it! They've been together since practically the turn of the century."

Solemnly I said, "They're deep in love. Darren's the only boyfriend Frizz has ever had. I think she may be the only girlfriend *he's* ever had. They go everywhere together."

"Awesome," said Chloe.

"I know." I giggled. "Keri says they're like an old married couple."

"*Aaaaahhh!*"

We both made gurgling noises.

"It is kind of sweet, though," said Chloe.

"Mm…I guess." Frizz was my oldest friend, and just at first, when she'd started going out with Darren and

I wasn't going out with anyone, I'd felt a bit excluded. But I'd got over all that. I could be genuinely glad for Frizz that she was so happy. Of course, it helped that I now had a boyfriend of my own – plus the fact that in all honesty I wouldn't have fancied Darren even if he'd been available. He probably wouldn't have fancied me, either. He and Frizz were just, like, soul mates. The ideal couple!

"They're going to run a restaurant together," I said. "They've got it all planned."

"Wow." Chloe slid both hands beneath her thighs and rocked, thoughtfully. We were sitting on a bench in the sunshine, during lunch break, waiting for Katie and Chantal to join us. The conversation, as usual, had turned to our favourite subject: *boys*. There had once been a time, back in Year 7, when Chloe and I had earnestly and at great length discussed books, and school, and homework. We still occasionally discussed books, cos it's fun if you've read the same ones and you can compare notes and talk about your favourite characters; but we hardly ever discussed school or homework any more. It was always boys. Boys we fancied, boys we didn't fancy; boys we'd like to kiss, boys we wouldn't touch with a barge pole. We were obsessed by the opposite sex!

"How about Lily?" Chloe stopped rocking and tipped backwards, her legs stuck out in front of her. She'd overbalance if she wasn't careful. "Has she got anyone yet?"

I said, "Lily's mad about this boy in her dancing class...Joel? He's her partner – they do *pas de deux* together. *Swan Lake* and stuff. I'm not sure you could actually call him her boyfriend, cos they don't really go on dates. But she's working on it."

"'Bout time," said Chloe.

"That's what Keri says. She also says Joel's bound to be gay, just cos he's a dancer. It really upsets Lily."

"*Is* he?"

I said, "Who cares? He's still gorgeous! Anyway, Keri hasn't even met him, so what would she know?"

"She knows everything," said Chloe.

"She thinks she does." Chloe was quoting something I'd told her ages ago. Keri is not only a know-all, she's also incredibly bossy. But she does have her good points. She's very generous, for a start. Her mum and dad are quite rich, which means that Keri has oceans of pocket money and a wardrobe bulging with designer clothes. But she doesn't boast about it, and she's always willing to share and to give you stuff. Jewellery and make-up, stuff like that.

"So who's she going out with?"

I humped a shoulder. "Damian? Charlie? Leo? Who knows? I can't keep up with her. It seems to be someone different every week."

Chloe nodded. "She's playing the field."

"Dunno about that. *She* says they keep making

demands...wanting things she's not prepared to give."

"In that case," said Chloe, "she's sending out the wrong messages."

"You mean, like, she flirts."

Darkly Chloe said, "There's another name for it. It's not fair to lead boys on."

I thought to myself that I wouldn't know *how* to lead a boy on, even if I wanted to. But I didn't say so in case it made me seem babyish.

"You still going out with Rees?" said Chloe.

"Mm." I bent my head to hide the stupid blush that came over me. Blushing is *really* babyish.

"I s'pose he's your hero now," said Chloe. "After giving you the kiss of life."

That made me blush even more. "It was only for a wasp sting," I muttered. "It wasn't a heart attack or anything. I was just allergic."

"But you'd stopped breathing! Not every boy would try kissing you back to life... D'you think you'd have done it to him?"

I wanted to say, *Yes, of course I would!* I mean, it's what everybody would do if they thought someone had stopped breathing. *Everybody except me.* But I didn't have to go and say so! It seems there are times when, for some idiotic reason I don't understand, I feel compelled to utter the truth.

"I'm not sure I'd know how," I said.

"Me neither!" Chloe looked at me, wide-eyed. "Isn't it awful? We'd let people *die*!"

It was a sobering thought, and one I didn't care to dwell on. Sometimes I am just so inadequate I frighten myself.

"I might do it for Bundle," I said. Bundle is my dog. Oh, God! That was even worse. I'd for it for Bundle and not for Rees??? "I mean—" What did I mean? "It wouldn't be so embarrassing," I said. "You know, if I did it wrong."

Chloe didn't sneer, as Keri might have done. She nodded and said, "I know what you mean."

I really didn't want to talk about it any more. Rushing back to the safer subject of boys, I said, "We're all planning to go out one day soon as a foursome. With our boyfriends! Keri's going to arrange it. We thought we might go to Hastings, cos that's where her school is. Then we could go round town, and go to the beach, and go on the pier. If they have a pier. I'm really looking forward to it."

"Oh!" Chloe gasped. "That sounds brilliant! Can I come with you?"

I said, "Um…" and then stopped. I think I must have left my mouth hanging open, cos she hastened on reassure me that she wouldn't just tag along like a beetroot. (I don't know why she said beetroot; I think she meant gooseberry. Gooseberry is what it's called

13

when you're the odd one out.) Anyway, she promised that she'd bring a boyfriend with her.

"I could ask Danny! You know, Danny MacIntyre that lives in my road? We could be a fivesome!"

There was a moment of horrible silence; I just didn't know what to say. Lily, and Keri, and Frizz, and me, we'd all grown up together. We'd been at juniors together. Even though we'd all moved on to different schools – Lily at her dancing school, Keri at boarding school, me at Rosemount, Frizz at Heathfield – we were still the Gang of Four. Outsiders didn't really fit in. They didn't understand our private jokes! Like, if one of us should suddenly say, *pink knickers*, in these really scathing tones, the others would immediately know we were referring to a particularly hideous girl called Jessamy James that used to be at juniors with us. Chloe would know that she was hideous, because everybody who met her knew that; but she wouldn't know that Jessamy had once been shameless enough to do handstands in the playground, in front of absolutely everybody, and we had *all seen her knickers*. Pale repulsive pink. Yuck!

Keri had once invited one of her posh friends, Mima, to join us (Mima being short for Jemima, if you can believe that). It had totally ruined everything. I didn't for one minute imagine that Chloe would ruin things, since unlike Mima she is not at all a superior, showing-off kind of person. *She* doesn't keep drawling and posturing and

14

flinging her hair back. Well, she couldn't fling her hair back, as she has it cut very short, in spikes, and she certainly doesn't drawl. On the contrary, she speaks very fast, shooting words out of her mouth like a hail of machine-gun bullets. The teachers are always telling her, "Chloe, don't gabble!" At school she is my *very best friend,* but that still didn't make her one of us.

She stood there, eagerly waiting for me to reply. I could see her bright hopeful smile gradually start to fade as she realised I was searching for a way out. I felt terrible. I had to say something! But what? Fortunately, it was at this point that Chantal and Katie arrived. They were bubbling over with some story about how a girl in our class, Lettuce, had gone and got herself locked in the girls' loo.

"She was there all morning. I know it's not funny" – Katie stuffed her hand into her mouth to stop herself laughing – "but trust Lettuce!"

"I'd have climbed out," said Chantal.

"Anyone would!"

"'Cept Lettuce."

"She is a bit wet," I said. "When I first started here she kind of clung to me like a damp leaf."

"She *is* a damp leaf!"

The conversation surged off in a different direction, everyone telling stories about poor old Lettuce and how dismal she was. *I was saved! For the moment.* After,

I agonised all through maths, wondering what excuse I could make that wouldn't be hurtful, but in the end Chloe solved the problem for me.

"Look, it's OK," she said. "I shouldn't have asked. I know you like to do things in a bunch."

Awkwardly I said, "It's just...if we all invited other people—"

"I know," said Chloe. "It's OK! Honest." And then she gave one of her toothy grins and said, "Your maths is way out, by the way...*foursome*. It's an eightsome!"

I didn't remind her that she had suggested making it a fivesome; it wouldn't have been kind. Not when she was being so nice about it all. I just meekly agreed that maths was not my best subject.

"You can say that again!" said Chloe. She is allowed to say these things; she herself is some kind of mathematical genius. I, on the other hand, am still at the stage of counting on my fingers. "Tell you what!" She linked her arm through mine, to show there were no hard feelings. "Maybe one day you and me could go somewhere with Danny and Rees and *really* be a foursome?"

I said that I would like that, thinking to myself that Chloe was a *true* friend. I still felt a bit guilty, however.

As soon as we were let out of school I checked my mobile for messages. I was hoping there might be something from Keri, fixing a date for our outing. I was just *so* looking forward to it! It was ages since the four of us had been anywhere or done anything together. We'd certainly never done anything as an eightsome...with boyfriends!

There wasn't anything from Keri – just a text from Lily, saying *Call me.* I tried, but she wasn't answering. Then I remembered that she had dance classes until quite late on a Friday, so I left a message and went racing back home to see if Keri might perhaps have emailed me. She hadn't. I asked Mum, "Keri didn't ring, did she?"

Mum said, "No, why would she ring here? Surely she'd use your mobile?"

"I just wondered," I said.

So then I rang Frizz, to see if she'd heard anything. She said she hadn't.

"She's leaving it so late!" I said. "It'll be half-term in a couple of weeks."

"Oh, well, you know Keri." Frizz didn't sound very concerned. "Leaves everything till the last minute."

"Problems?" said Mum, as I wandered into the kitchen.

"No, I'm just waiting for Keri to fix a date for our outing."

Craig was in the kitchen, stuffing biscuits into his mouth. He's my brother, but more often behaves like some kind of warthog. He said, "What outing?" I dodged a spray of biscuit crumbs. Talk about repulsive!

"Do you have to speak with your mouth full?" I said.

Craig chewed, and swallowed. I saw his Adam's apple bounce up and down. "For your information," he said, "I'm training myself. Time is money. You have to learn to multi-task if you want to get anywhere."

"Don't see where spitting's going to get you!"

"I won't spit once I've trained myself. Everybody has to learn. What's all this about an outing?"

"If you must know," I said, "though it's no business of yours, we're going to Hastings for the day."

"All of them," said Mum. "With their boyfriends. Should be fun!"

Craig stuffed another couple of biscuits into his mouth. "Oo gownith nix?"

Well, that's what it sounded like. I translated it as, "You going with Knickers?" Knickers is his *ultra* annoying way of referring to Rees. Just cos Rees's surname is Nicholson. I ignored him; sometimes it's the only thing to do. I turned to Mum.

"Chloe asked me if she could come with us."

"That would be nice," said Mum. "A big group of you." I frowned.

"What's the matter? Don't you want her to go?"

"She wouldn't really fit in."

"No?"

"I've known the others so long!"

"Well, it's up to you," said Mum. "Have you told her?"

"She's OK. She understands."

18

"If Knickers is going, I don't see why I shouldn't, too," said Craig.

He and Rees are in the same class at St Henry's. I personally think it would be purgatory being in the same class as Craig – being in the same *school* as Craig – but Rees says he's not actually that bad. He reckons he just likes to wind me up.

"Why can't I come?" he said.

"Cos you'd be a gooseberry!"

"What's that s'posed to mean?"

I said, "Odd man out."

"Yeah? Well, that's where you're wrong, cos I'd bring my girlfriend!"

I looked at him suspiciously. "Not that Darcie creature?"

"Nah! She's history. Got someone else now. Someone classy. Goes to your school… Sam Matthewson?"

"Never heard of her."

"That's cos she's in Year *10*. Doesn't mix with the likes of you."

"In that case she's too old and we don't want her. This is just for *us*. If Chloe can't come, neither can you."

"I don't think they should be allowed to go, anyway," said Craig. He appealed to Mum. "You know what girls are like… They'll get all drunk and stupid and roar about the place upsetting people."

"*I beg your pardon*," I said. "I am not the one that

19

gets drunk and spends half the night with his head stuffed down the toilet bowl!"

Craig's face turned a mottled shade of purple. I felt a bit mean, but not very. He hurled the empty biscuit packet into the sink and wrenched open the back door, yelling at Bundle to follow him. As he slammed the door behind him he yelled, "That was at Christmas, you blithering idiot!"

"Like that makes it OK?" I shrieked. *"Honestly.* That boy has some nerve!"

Mum shook her head. "I can't help wondering," she said, "whether some people are lucky enough to have children who love each other?"

I do love Craig, deep down. It's just that he does my head in!

"You shouldn't let him get to you," said Mum. "And it wasn't quite fair, bringing up Christmas."

"His behaviour was disgusting."

"Boys will be boys... He was just experimenting. Sometimes you have to learn the hard way."

It wasn't any excuse! Rees wouldn't behave like that. Going round emptying all the glasses when people's backs were turned. Wine, and gin, and Gran's eggnog. Not to mention Dad's whisky! No wonder he spent the night in the bathroom. The really maddening thing, according to Dad, was that he didn't wake up with a hangover.

"Oh, Polly!" Mum laughed. "Try to be a little charitable... Is that your phone? Maybe it's the call you've been waiting for."

"Keri!"

But it wasn't Keri, it was Lily. She sounded agitated.

Chapter 2

"Polly?"

I said, "Yes?"

"It's Lily."

"Yes."

"I need to talk!"

I said, "Right."

There was a pause.

"I mean, like, *talk*," said Lily.

"OK!" I settled myself comfortably at the foot of the stairs, leaning back against the wall. I waited.

"No, I mean, talk properly!"

What was she saying, *talk properly*? I frowned into the telephone. This wasn't like Lily. What was wrong?

"You can talk," I said.

"Not on the phone! Can I come round?"

"What, like, now?"

"*Please!*" She was sounding increasingly desperate.

"I won't stay long, if you want to go out with Rees or anything."

"That's all right," I said. "Rees is away for the weekend. I'm not going anywhere."

"So can I come? I'm on my way home – I'll be at the station in five minutes. I could come straight over. I'll just ring Mum and tell her. Is that OK?"

Of course, I said yes. I couldn't help being curious, but also a bit worried. Lily is not the sort of person to go round splurging over people or to throw hissy fits. She is quite self-contained. I couldn't imagine what had happened to upset her. The worst I could think of was that she'd been thrown out of her dancing school. I knew, because Lily had told us, that they did throw people out, like if they got too tall or too fat, or just weren't reaching a high enough standard. "They're absolutely ruthless!" she had said.

It would break Lily's heart if she were thrown out; dancing was her entire life. But why would she want to come and talk to me about it, rather than Keri? It had always been me and Frizz, Lily and Keri.

I rushed back out to the kitchen and said, "Lily's coming round."

"Right," said Mum. "Do you want to take some stuff upstairs with you?"

I grabbed a handful of grapes and some flapjacky things with nuts and raisins, plus a couple of cans of

Coke, and whizzed them up to my bedroom. In spite of hovering near the window, keeping watch, I was still beaten to the front door by Craig. Goodness knows what he was doing there. He said, "Hi, Lily!" and stood beaming, looking foolish. I grabbed hold of Lily and hustled her in.

"'Scuse us," I said, "we have things to talk about."

Lily wouldn't eat any of the food I'd got for her. Not even the flapjacks, which she normally loves. She just shook her head and said she couldn't.

"I'm not hungry."

"So what is it?" I said. "What's happened?"

She hurled herself onto my bed. "Keri was right!"

Cautiously I said, "Right about what?"

"Joel!" She snatched up a pillow and sat there, clutching it to her chest. (I can't call it her bosom cos she hasn't got any. She's tiny as a matchstick.) She looked up at me tragically. "He's gay!"

I said, "Oh." And then, "How did you find out?"

"Cos he told me!"

"What, he actually said to you that he was gay?"

"He told me he fancies this boy in Year 11!"

"Gosh." It was all I could immediately think of to say. *Not* very helpful. I racked my brains for something a bit more intelligent. "Maybe it's just...a phase he's going through." It's what one of my grans always says, whenever me and Craig get some kind of new

24

enthusiasm going. Like when Craig was mad to try skydiving, or I wanted to enrol at a modelling agency (ha ha! What a joke!). *It's just a phase they're going through*, she says.

Quite often, though I hate to admit it, she turns out to be right. But Lily shook her head, quite violently. "It's not a phase! He told me...he's been crazy about this boy for months! He said I was the only person he could confide in. He asked me" – she rocked distractedly, to and fro – "whether I thought he ought to say something."

"What, to this boy?"

"Whether he should tell him how he felt."

"What did you say?"

"I said, yes, go for it! What else could I say?"

"So has he?"

"He's going to. This weekend."

"Maybe..." I suddenly saw a chink of light. "Maybe the boy will say he doesn't want to know cos he's got a girlfriend."

"He hasn't got a girlfriend! He's gay, too."

"Ah. Mm." Yes, well. I had the feeling I wasn't being very supportive. "It doesn't stop you being partners," I said brightly. Lily had once told us that that was the most important thing. "You can still dance together. It doesn't make any difference there, does it?"

Lily shrugged. "S'pose not."

"So that's one thing!" I said.

She gazed at me tragically. "It won't be the same." Her face crumpled. "He'll never be my boyfriend!"

"He might be," I said.

"How? How could he be?"

"Well…I dunno! Like…if he grows out of it, or something."

Lily didn't say anything to this.

"People do," I said. "I'm sure they do. I read about it somewhere." Or was I just making that up? I did so want to find *something* positive to say! I'd never seen Lily in tears before. Back in primary school, me and Frizz were for ever grizzling over something or other – some girl had been nasty to us, or a teacher had been mean. The least little thing set us off. Even Keri had had a bit of a wail when she tripped over in the playground and broke her arm. But never Lily. The only time Lily ever gave way to her emotions was when she was dancing.

"Thing is," I said, "look at it this way – it could be worse. He could fancy another girl! I mean, goodness, if Rees started fancying someone else I'd far rather it was a boy."

"Why?" said Lily.

"Well, because…it wouldn't be so insulting."

Tears dripped miserably off Lily's cheeks. "I'm not ever going to find anyone else!"

"Course you are," I said. "You've got all your life ahead of you."

Another of Gran's sayings. It drives me completely

nuts, so why I went and said it to Lily I really can't imagine. I was supposed to be comforting her, not adding to her distress. She was sobbing now.

"I don't want anyone else! I just want Joel!"

I gave her a box of tissues and waited, sympathetically, while she blew her nose and dried herself up.

"I'm sorry I'm being so silly," she said.

I told her that she wasn't being silly. I said, "Falling in love is one of life's big experiences."

Lily dabbed at her eyes. "Are you in love with Rees?"

I hesitated; I knew I had to answer honestly. "I'd like to be," I said, "cos I'd like to know what it feels like. Sometimes I pretend that I am…like, if I try hard enough I can make it happen. But I don't think it's the same as what you feel for Joel. It's not a grand passion." Lily looked pleased at that. She liked the idea that she had a grand passion. "I do enjoy being with him, though."

"Yes." Lily sighed, and nodded. "It's probably less painful that way. I'd better be getting back, I promised Mum I wouldn't stay long. Thank you for letting me talk."

"'S all right," I said. "It's what friends are for."

She gave me a watery smile. "Don't say anything to Keri, will you? I know she'll have to know some time, but I don't want her saying I told you so."

I thought she was being a bit unfair on Keri. However bossy and opinionated she might be, she never crows or gloats.

27

As we went downstairs, I said anxiously, "You'll still be OK for Hastings?"

"I can't come to Hastings *now*," said Lily.

I didn't see why not; she and Joel were still partners. They were still friends! But I let the subject drop as it didn't seem quite the right moment.

Craig was hovering in the hall. "Leaving already?" he said.

"She has to get back." I pushed past him and practically shoved Lily through the door. Being bothered by Craig was the last thing she needed.

Craig leaned out and bellowed after her. "Dad and me'll give you a lift, if you like!"

"She doesn't want a lift," I said.

"How d'you know?"

"Cos she's upset. She doesn't want to talk to people."

"What's she upset about?"

"If you must know," I said, "she's having boyfriend problems."

"What, like, they've split?" He didn't have to sound so *gleeful.*

"Something like that."

Mum appeared in the hall. "Lily gone?" She sounded surprised. "That was quick!"

"She's upset," said Craig. "She's broken up with her boyfriend."

"Oh, dear! Poor Lily. Is she taking it very hard?"

"She doesn't think she'll be able to come on our outing," I said.

"Well, that's a shame, but she wouldn't want to be the only one on her own."

"I could go with her," said Craig.

I said, "*You*?"

"Why not? I like Lily."

He was serious! I realised, looking back, that he had always been quite sweet on her. "But you've already got a girlfriend," I said.

"Yeah, well...sort of. Needn't stop me seeing Lily."

"You are *not* playing one girl off against the other," said Mum. "That is definitely not on."

"All right, I'd junk one! Not Lily." He grinned. He actually *grinned*. "The other one!"

Mum shook her head. "There are times," she said, "when I despair."

When Mum disappeared upstairs, Craig said, "Well? What d'you reckon? Would she like me to go with her?" I was on the point of saying *she doesn't hang out with warthogs*, when in these almost humble tones, he added, "I'd like it."

It sort of took the wind out of my sails, as the saying goes.

"You could always ask her for me," said Craig.

I hesitated; then said OK, I would ask her. It's true I wouldn't want to go out with Craig *myself*, but then of

29

course he is my brother. Other girls might see him differently. They might even think he wasn't too bad-looking. I mean, he's not positively ugly, and he doesn't have spots. And going with Craig had to be better than not going at all. Lily had been looking forward to our outing as much as I had! She couldn't really want to miss out.

"So you gonna do it, then?" he asked.

"*Yes.* I just said."

"So what you waiting for?"

"I'm not doing it right away! She won't even be back home yet."

"She's got a mobile, hasn't she?"

"She'll be sitting on a *bus*," I said. "She doesn't want to talk about things while she's sitting on a bus!"

"Why not?"

"God," I cried, "you are *so* insensitive!"

"I just want to get it settled. I need to know where I am. How long's it take her to get home?"

"I don't know! 'Bout twenty minutes."

"And then she'll need to have her tea," said Mum.

"If she's eating. She's probably too upset."

"That's why you got to ring her," said Craig. "She'll feel better when she knows I'm willing to go out with her."

Mum and I exchanged glances. Mum rolled her eyes. I thought, *Boys!* Well, no, that wasn't fair – they weren't all like that. Rees wasn't, for instance. Craig is just one of those maddening people who one minute is being all pathetic and makes you feel sorry for him, and the next he goes and blows it and gets you into a state of absolute rage. I told him I would ring Lily *later.*

"Well, don't leave it too long," said Craig, "I'm calling round for Sam at seven o'clock."

You see? That's exactly what I'm talking about!

At half-past six he started nagging me. Dad had come in, and wanted to know what all the excitement was about.

"It's just Craig," I said. "He wants to find out who's going to have the honour of being his girlfriend, and which one he's going to junk."

"I wouldn't junk Lily," said Craig.

"I wouldn't junk Lily," said Dad. He gave Craig the thumbs-up. "Go for it – I would!"

"I'm trying to," said Craig, "but she won't ring her."

"Oh, all *right,*" I said. "Don't keep on! I'll go and do it – but upstairs, cos I don't want you perving in the background!"

Lily sounded a bit breathless as she answered the phone, as if she'd been in the garden and had rushed indoors in a flurry.

"'Lo?"

"It's only me," I said.

"Oh! Polly. Hi."

I could feel her disappointment coming at me in great waves. She'd hoped I was going to be Joel! I almost wished I hadn't rung. It's cruel to raise people's expectations.

"Sorry," I said.

"'S all right."

"Have you heard from him?"

"No." Bravely she added, "I'm not really expecting to. He'll probably call tomorrow to tell me how things went."

Like whether the boy he was crazy about was crazy about him. I sighed. How complicated it was, having a love life!

"Reason I'm ringing...Craig wondered, when we go to Hastings, whether he could come with us. Like, with you."

"*Craig*?" Lily seemed slightly taken aback, which wasn't really surprising considering the number of times I'd complained about him.

"I know I'm always saying what a pain he is, but he's only a pain if you're his sister. He's mostly OK with other people. I mean, he can actually be quite nice with other people. And he really likes you!"

Lily didn't say anything to this.

"Honestly," I said, "I think he's got a thing about you...he was practically begging me to ring. He's not brave enough to do it himself."

Still nothing.

I ploughed on. "I know he's not as gorgeous as Joel, but he'd be on his best behaviour, I promise! Cos Rees would be there and they're sort of, like, friends. It'll be such fun, all of us together! You can't not come."

There was a choking sound at the other end of the phone.

"Lily?"

"I'm sorry, but if I can't go with Joel" – her voice rose to a wail – "I don't want to go with anyone!" She had it really bad; I knew there wasn't any point in trying to persuade her. Slowly, I went back downstairs.

Craig said, "Well?"

I shook my head. "She says if she can't go with Joel, she doesn't want to go with anyone."

Craig's face grew red and hot. He said, "What kind of sense does that make?"

"Every sense, if she loves him," said Mum.

"Yeah? Well, he obviously doesn't love her!"

"He does, in his own way," I said. "Just not the way she wants him to."

"What's that s'posed to mean?"

"He's gay," I said.

"Well, that's even stupider!" roared Craig.

"No, it's not," said Mum. "You can't help who you fall in love with – and you can't just fall out of love at a moment's notice. She needs time. Don't rush her!"

"She's feeling specially bad about it," I said, "cos

33

Keri's been saying all along he's bound to be gay. She just didn't want to believe it."

Craig made a rude honking noise down his nose.

"Not that Keri's ever met him," I said.

"So why did she think he had to be gay?" asked Mum.

"Oh, just cos he's a dancer."

Dad chuckled. "Our Keri sounds like a woman of the world!"

"Sounds somewhat prejudiced to me," said Mum.

"Oh, come on!" said Dad. "Let's face it…not exactly what you'd call a manly profession, is it?"

"It's girly," said Craig.

"That's one way of putting it."

"It's no way of putting it!" Mum spoke sharply. "You make me ashamed, the pair of you!"

Dad held up his hands. "Just joking. Don't shoot!"

"It *is* girly," said Craig. "Poncing about in tights…*bluuurgh*!"

Whatever that meant. I guessed he was only doing it because of feeling hurt and rejected, but any sort of prejudice gets Mum really mad. She told Craig that he had an attitude.

"You've got it from your father! He has an attitude, as well. You both seem to think it's clever to jeer at anyone who's not exactly the same as you are!"

"Hey, whoa, steady on," said Dad. He cringed back on his chair in mock terror, but Mum wasn't laughing. She'd got the bit between her teeth and was well away.

"I thought this kind of thing went out with the ark! You're like a couple of throwbacks. You sit there, all smug and complacent—"

"I'm going to ring Frizz," I said. I pushed back my chair. Nobody took any notice. Probably nobody even heard me. I went back up to my room and called Frizz's number.

"Oh, good, you're there," I said as she answered. "I thought you might be out."

"Going out any minute," said Frizz. "Melanie Philpotts is having a party. Darren's coming to pick me up."

"Lucky you! Rees is away for the weekend."

"Feel like coming over Sunday?"

I said, "I'd love to! Then you can give me all the goss." And then, without even *trying* to stop myself, I said, "I've got goss!"

"Mm?" Frizz made encouraging noises down the telephone.

"Lily," I said. "She's in a terrible state...she's just discovered that Keri's been right all along."

Frizz guessed at once what I was talking about. "Joel? He's gay?"

"He's deep in love with another boy."

"Oh! Poor Lily."

"I know, she's ever so upset."

"I can imagine. She was mad about him!"

"Now she says she won't be coming on our outing. Craig offered to go with her but she says if she can't go with Joel she doesn't want to go with anyone."

"Well, I s'pose there's nothing to stop him coming with her – Joel, I mean."

"If he's not too busy mooning about over this other boy."

"Mm. That would make it kind of awkward."

"It would be horrible for her! I think she ought to come with Craig. She can't *not* come."

"Well, maybe she'll change her mind. Hey, I gotta go, Darren's here! See you tomorrow. 'Bout eleven?"

"Yes, fine. Oh, and Frizz! Don't tell Keri, will you? Lily doesn't want her knowing."

She hadn't actually asked me not to tell Frizz, which surely she would have done if she hadn't wanted me to. She knew that me and Frizz tell each other everything.

"I won't say a word," Frizz promised. "Anyway, why would I be talking to Keri?"

"Well, you know…if she rang about the outing, or something."

I wandered back downstairs to find that Mum and Dad had made up. They never stay cross with each other for long. I said to Craig that Frizz thought it was possible Lily might change her mind about going to Hastings with him. "She just needs a bit of time."

Craig said, "Might be too late by then."

36

"Why?" I said. "What's going to happen?"

"Might have decided I prefer Sam." He is the *most* annoying boy.

"You can't hurry these things," I said. "You've obviously never been in love."

"Don't wanna be, neither," said Craig. "Not if it turns your brains to mush."

Absolutely *the* most annoying.

Chapter 3

Next morning I had a text from Rees saying he would be back by lunchtime and maybe we could meet up in the park later on with the dogs. That is, my dog Bundle and his dog Rufus. He said, *2.30 OK?*

I immediately texted back to say yes. I was pleased with the suggestion; it meant my diary was satisfyingly full. I like it when my diary is full. I think it's so pathetic when the pages remain blank. I'd already written "FRIZZ 11 O'CLOCK" in big red letters; now I had "REES 2.30". Yesterday there had been "LILY COMING OVER". This was good! Anyone nosy enough to pry would see that I was fully booked.

Dad said that if I liked he would give me a lift into town, to Frizz's place. "Just let me finish this job for your mum or I'll be in trouble."

"Yes, you will," said Mum. "That tap's been leaking for days!"

Dad pulled his henpecked face and disappeared under the sink with a wrench. Or maybe it was a spanner – I'm not sure I know the difference. While I was waiting for him, my phone rang. I thought it would be Keri with arrangements for our outing, and wondered if I should tell her that Lily might not be coming – though of course I wouldn't say why. I would pretend not to know. But anyway, it wasn't Keri, it was Chloe, sounding very full of herself.

"We're going to Brighton!" she said.

I asked, "Who is?"

"Me and the others…Katie and Chantal. Plus boyfriends!" She giggled happily. "We've just fixed it up."

"OK." I said it slowly, trying to give myself time to think. What could have made her ring up to tell me something that could easily have waited till we saw each other at school the next day? And why did she have to sound so triumphant? Almost like she was gloating. Rather coldly, I said, "When are you going?"

"Next Saturday. We're catching the train at *nine o'clock* and we're not coming back till six! We chose Brighton cos it's where Katie's boyfriend lives and it's, like, more fun than Hastings."

I bristled at that. "Hastings is fun!" I said. Not that I'd ever been there.

"Yes, but Brighton is *more* fun." Chloe giggled again.

"Brighton's wicked! In any case, it's easier to get to. Only takes twenty minutes."

"So does Hastings."

"No, it doesn't! Hastings takes over an hour. You have to change trains. I looked it up."

I was beginning to feel decidedly prickly. I didn't like the idea of them all plotting and planning behind my back – *going off without me.* Chloe was supposed to be my best friend! My best school friend. And Katie and Chantal were my second-best school friends. How could they go off for the day and not include me???

Chloe, as if reading my mind, said, "I'm afraid I can't really invite you to come with us."

Why couldn't she?

"See, Katie's boyfriend and Chantal's boyfriend and my boyfriend are all best mates."

Oh? I thought. Aloud, I said "So who's your boyfriend? I thought you were going to ask that one that lives in your road."

"Danny – yes. I decided against it. Katie says this boy that's best mates with her and Chantal's boyfriends is really, really nice, so I'm going to go with him."

"You mean a blind date?" I could hear the disapproval oozing prudishly out of my mouth.

"Why not? Never get anywhere if you're not prepared to take chances."

I thought to myself that this was one of my problems:

40

I am almost never prepared to take chances. I am not brave enough. I have this morbid sort of mind that always imagines the worst.

"Anyway, I'm really sorry I can't ask you," said Chloe. "It's just that with the boys all knowing each other—"

"That's all right," I said. "I'm already going to Hastings. I wouldn't want to go to Brighton as well."

"No, well, this is it," said Chloe. "I'll go to Brighton, and you go to Hastings, and then we can compare notes! When are you actually going?"

"Might be the same day as you," I said.

"Ooh, we could text each other! Like, *I'm on the pier, where are you?* That'd be fun!"

I said that it would, trying – but not very hard – to sound enthusiastic. Truth be told, I was glad that at that point Dad stuck his head round the door and said, "OK?" and I was able to tell Chloe that I had to go. I wouldn't have wanted to quarrel with her, cos Chloe and me don't do quarrels, but I was feeling quite resentful. She'd stolen *my* idea and gone and set it all up with *my* friends, and didn't seem to see anything wrong in it! Me not inviting her to come to Hastings was totally, utterly different, and she must know that it was. Well, she did know! She'd told me so herself; she'd said she understood. People, I thought, were such a disappointment.

I grumbled to Dad about it as we drove into town. Dad said it was always a problem when you kept your friends in separate compartments.

"You do some things with one lot, and some things with another, and it all works out fine until suddenly they clash and that's it, you're in trouble!"

"I'm not in *trouble*," I said. "I just don't see why she couldn't have asked me!"

But I wasn't going to moan to Frizz about it. Me and Frizz were going to spend a pleasant couple of hours gossiping! We hadn't had a good gossiping session for simply ages. We hardly ever seemed to get together any more. In the old days, hardly a week had gone by without Frizz staying at my place or me staying at hers, but I couldn't remember the last time that had happened. Perhaps, I thought sadly, we were too old for sleepovers. But not too old for a heart-to-heart!

"So, what's the goss?" I said, as we went upstairs to Frizz's bedroom. Frizz's mum and dad run a newsagent's, which has this tiny little poky flat above it. If you were a huge hulking sort of person you would have to turn sideways to get up the stairs, they're so narrow. And Frizz's bedroom is a bit like a room in a doll's house. In the past, when sometimes we had all met up there, we could only just about manage to squeeze ourselves in. But oh, we had such good times! Every bit as good as in Keri's posh bedroom, which is almost as big as an entire apartment. These days, Keri's was generally the only place we ever got together.

"So what's the goss?" I repeated, settling myself comfortably on Frizz's bed and preparing for a cosy chat. "What's new?"

Frizz said, "Nothing much. Tell me about Lily. I want to hear about Lily!" She plumped herself down on the floor. "What exactly happened?"

"Well, I'm not sure *exactly*," I said, "but it seems like Keri's turned out to be right—"

"He's been gay all along!"

"Seems so."

"He finally admitted it!"

"Well…" I hesitated. I didn't think *admitted* was quite the right word. When you admit something it's like you're ashamed, or guilty. Like you've done something wrong. Joel hadn't done anything wrong.

"He told her," prompted Frizz.

"Yes." I thought back, trying to remember all that Lily had said. She'd been so upset that it had all come pouring out in a great incoherent splurge. "He told her he was in love with this other boy."

"Which boy?"

"I don't know which boy. Just some boy at their school. I think he's in the class above theirs."

"What does Lily think of him?"

"Of the boy? She didn't say."

"Does she hate him?"

"N-no. I don't think so."

"She ought to," Frizz said vehemently. "I would!"

I stared at her, bemused. "Why?"

"Stealing him from her."

"But he didn't steal him! He didn't even know. It wasn't his fault."

"Course it was! These things don't just happen by accident."

"Sometimes they do."

"If you believe that, you'll believe anything," said Frizz. "I bet he'd been making eyes at him for weeks, trying to get his attention."

"You mean…" I wasn't sure that I knew what she was talking about. "You mean, the boy had been making eyes at Joel, or Joel had been making eyes at him?"

"Both, probably!"

I fell silent.

"Well, go on!" said Frizz. "What else?"

"There isn't anything else. That's all she told me. Oh, except Joel's going to say something this weekend."

"To the boy?"

"Yes. And then he's going to report back to Lily."

Frizz was leaning forward, listening intently. It was like she couldn't get enough. Like she just wanted to keep me talking. Every time I thought I'd come to the end, she'd find yet another question.

"So what d'you think Lily's going to do?"

I said, "Well, they'll still be friends. They'll still be

44

partners. It doesn't alter that."

"But will she still love him?"

"She does at the moment."

"Even though he's betrayed her?"

I gazed at Frizz doubtfully.

Angrily she said, "He should have told her ages ago! It was cruel, just letting her go on."

"Maybe he didn't realise."

"Didn't realise he was gay?" She sounded scornful.

I said, "He might not have done. People don't always; it's something you have to discover." But that wasn't what I'd meant. "Even if he had realised," I said, "he mightn't have known how Lily felt about him."

Frizz frowned, like she didn't want to accept that. "They dance love scenes together!"

"That's just acting. Doesn't necessarily mean anything."

"I don't care! He should still have told her."

"You mean, if he'd realised."

"Course he realised! You said he'd been crazy about this other boy for ages."

"I didn't say for ages!" That was just Frizz's interpretation. "I don't know how long he's been crazy about him. It might have only just happened."

Fiercely, Frizz said, "Why are you defending him?"

"Cos he hasn't done anything wrong!"

"You're only saying that cos you're half in love

with him yourself," said Frizz.

I felt my cheeks flare up. "Am not!"

Frizz looked at me with a kind of pitying contempt, like, how sad can you get? Fortunately, she didn't pursue the subject. She was more interested in having a go at Joel.

"He should have come out. Otherwise, it's deceitful." She sat up, very stiff and straight. "It's like living a lie. It's not fair on people!"

By people, I supposed she meant Lily. I couldn't help wondering why she was getting so uptight about it. It wasn't like Frizz to be judgemental.

I said, "He can't help the way he feels!"

"That's not the point! The point is, he led her on."

Oh dear, I thought. Frizz was becoming obsessed. She wasn't even talking sense. "I honestly don't think he did," I said. "I think she led herself on."

"That's right, blame Lily!"

"I'm not blaming her. I'm just saying—"

"You're just saying it's her fault for falling in love with him!"

"I'm saying *he didn't lead her on.*"

"How do you know?"

"Well, because…Lily would have said!"

"She might not have recognised the signs. She's never had a boyfriend before – she doesn't necessarily know what's normal. He obviously took advantage of her,

46

knowing all the time it wasn't going to go anywhere, and now look what's happened... He's gone and broken her heart and she'll probably never trust any boy ever again!" Frizz had jumped up and was banging noisily about the room. "It could have ruined her entire life!"

I fell silent; I didn't know what to say. I had the feeling that this strange conversation wasn't really about Joel and Lily – it was about something else. But I couldn't think what. Trying to lighten the mood I said brightly, "So, anyway! What happened at the party?"

Frizz spun round. Her eyes raked me accusingly. "What do you mean, what happened?"

"Well...you know! What's the goss? Hot goss! There's gotta be some!"

My efforts at encouragement fell flat. Frizz just scowled and set off again on her noisy banging. Something was obviously wrong. Frizz is not at all a temperamental sort of person, and she is never spiteful or ill-tempered.

"How was Darcie?" I said. "She was all done up like a daffodil last time I saw her! And d'you remember, at New Year's, how she looked like a Christmas tree? All covered in those stupid spangly things."

"Darcie White is a slag!" The words came bursting out. I was quite shocked. Not at what Frizz had said, cos I could have told her Darcie was a slag; but shocked that it was Frizz who was saying it. "She's a slimy, disgusting, two-timing *slag* and I don't want anything more to do with her!" Frizz snatched up a hairbrush and smashed it down, hard, on top of her dressing table. "I don't want anything more to do with Darren, either, so just don't talk to me about him! Don't even mention his name, cos I don't want to know. *OK*?"

I swallowed and said, "OK."

"And I'm not going to tell you anything more, so you can just shut up!"

Meekly, I did so. Frizz banged about a bit more, then flumped down onto the floor, rubbing her leg where she'd gone and crashed it into the wardrobe.

"If Craig wants to come to Hastings with me, he's welcome. I'm certainly not going with Darren. I'm not going anywhere with Darren! And if Lily doesn't want to go with him – with Craig, I mean—" She stopped, and glared at me. "*Well?* Does she or doesn't she?"

"No, she doesn't," I said.

"OK! In that case, you can tell him…I don't mind going with him. I don't see why I should miss out just because certain people can't behave themselves."

I was almost beside myself with curiosity, wondering what on earth could have happened, but I didn't dare ask. I'd never seen Frizz like this. It was difficult, in the circumstances, to find anything to talk about, so after a bit I said that I'd better be getting back.

"Don't forget to tell Craig I don't mind going

with him," said Frizz.

I promised that I would give him the message and went off to catch my bus, wondering who I could possibly ring to find out what had gone on at the party. Who did I know who might have been there?

I suddenly thought of someone: Melanie Philpotts! She had been at primary school with us and was now with Frizz at Heathfield. We'd been quite close at one time, though she'd never been part of the gang; but I might have kept her number. Yay! I had. I rang it at once, while I was waiting for the bus.

"Mel?"

"Polly." She didn't sound particularly surprised to hear from me. Maybe she'd been half-expecting it. "Are you ringing about Frizz?"

"Yes! What happened? She's in a terrible state. Something about Darren...she says she doesn't want anything more to do with him."

"I probably wouldn't, either," said Melanie, "if he was my boyfriend."

"Why? What did he do?"

"It was that Darcie...she made a pass at him."

"At *Darren*?" I know it was unworthy of me, but my immediate thought was, *why would Darcie make a pass at Darren*? He isn't at all the sort of boy she would normally go for. Much as I loathe and detest her, it has to be admitted that Darcie is quite attractive, in her own tacky way. So what would she want with Darren? And then, of course, it came to me: Darren belonged to Frizz. *That* was why she wanted him. It wouldn't be the first time she'd lured people's boyfriends away from them.

"They were in the kitchen," said Melanie. "Doing things."

I said, "*Doing* things?"

"Kissing. Cuddling."

"God!" I had to struggle to picture it. I just couldn't get my head round the idea of Darcie and Darren.

"It was awful," said Melanie. "Me and Frizz went out there to get something to drink and we caught them at it! Not that *she* cared." She meant Darcie. "She pretended to apologise, but you could tell she was enjoying herself. I bet she was just waiting for Frizz to walk in!"

"What about Darren? What did he do?"

"Nothing, he just stood there. He was really embarrassed! He went all red."

"Did he say anything?"

"No, cos Frizz didn't give him a chance. She went rushing out of the house. She must have gone home cos we didn't see her again. I was going to ring her, only I couldn't think what to say."

I couldn't think what to say, either. I could still hardly believe it. *Darren* making out with *Darcie. Darren* making out with *anybody.* He and Frizz had been together for so long! We were always joking about them being like an old married couple. How could he have done such a thing?

My bus arrived. I said a sober goodbye to Melanie, climbed up to the top deck and flung myself into the nearest seat. I found that I was quite glad to sit down. Everything was suddenly falling apart! First Lily, now Frizz. And me in the middle, like some kind of agony aunt.

Chapter 4

I thought that, before telling Craig he could come to Hastings with us, I really ought to do one last check with Lily. I mean, in case she might have changed her mind. Also, I felt that she ought to know about Frizz. After all, it wasn't like Frizz had sworn me to secrecy or anything.

I speed-dialled Lily's number as I sat on the bus.

"Lily, hi," I said. "Did you hear from Joel?"

"He just rang. A few minutes ago."

At least she wasn't sounding weepy, so there had obviously been a *slight* improvement.

"So what happened?" I said. "Did he go and see the boy?"

"Seth. Yes."

"And?"

"I'm not quite sure," said Lily, "but I don't think it went too well…he didn't sound very happy."

"You mean, Seth wasn't interested?"

"I think he's already got someone. But I don't really know." And then, in tones of quiet pride, she added, "We're going to talk about it tomorrow. After school. We're going for a coffee. Joel says I'm the only person he can confide in."

She'd told me that before; it was obviously important to her.

"I think that's really nice," I said. "Most boys don't ever discuss their feelings at all."

"Joel wouldn't with anyone else." Lily was quick to make it clear: she was the *only one*.

"It must mean you're very special to him," I said.

"We're partners," said Lily. "We understand each other."

"That's good! Anyway, look, the reason I'm ringing… I just wanted to make sure you hadn't changed your mind about Craig."

"*Polleee!*"

"I know, I know, but I had to ask. Cos if you *really* don't want to go to Hastings with him, I'm thinking he could go with Frizz."

"With *Frizz*? What about Darren?"

"Darren is a rat," I said. "She doesn't want anything more to do with him. *Or* with Darcie. He's a rat and she's a slag!"

Lily stifled a giggle; I knew, then, that she was starting to feel better. "What's going on?" she said.

53

I gave her all the details and we had a long, satisfying chat as I got off the bus and turned into Grange Road. Lily agreed that Darcie was hateful; but we also agreed that it had been Darren's fault as much as hers.

"There's no excuse," said Lily. "He didn't *have* to behave like that."

"He let himself be seduced," I said.

"I s'pose Darcie is quite sort of…prettyish."

"You mean *sexy.*"

"Slag-like!"

We giggled. I knew it wasn't really funny, but there are some words, you know you're not meant to use them, but when you do it just cracks you up.

"According to Mel," I said, "she deliberately set out to get him."

"It's what she does," said Lily.

"He can't really have thought she fancied him…honestly, boys are so *dumb!*"

"Some boys," said Lily. "Joel wouldn't behave like that."

"No," I said. "Rees wouldn't, either."

As soon as I got in, I went in search of Craig. I found him in the garden, kicking a ball for Bundle.

"Good news," I said. "You can come to Hastings, if you still want to."

"With Lily? She come to her senses?" *Maddening.* Absolutely *maddening.*

"With Frizz," I said.

Craig let out an indignant howl. "I don't wanna go with Frizz!"

"Well, you can't go with Lily cos she doesn't want to."

"Well, *I* don't wanna go with Frizz!"

"Why not?"

"Cos I don't fancy her!" roared Craig.

Mum, who was down on her knees yanking weeds out of a flowerbed, sat back on her heels and said, "Why isn't Frizz going with Darren?"

I told the story yet again (except I cut out the word *slag*). "It's that Darcie!" I said.

"Funny, isn't it," said Mum, "how it's always the woman that gets the blame?"

"Well, but, Mum, she did it on purpose! She deliberately set out to get him."

"Doesn't sound like he put up much of a fight."

"No, cos she *tempted* him."

"And men are such poor, weak, defenceless creatures."

"Hang about!" said Craig.

"I suppose you would have resisted?" said Mum.

I said, "Frizz would! She wouldn't ever be disloyal to Darren. She wouldn't go and kiss another boy!"

"Lucky if she got the chance," said Craig.

"You shut up!" I snarled. I felt like hitting him. I quite often feel like hitting him. He rouses these very violent

55

emotions in me. I try to be a pacifist, cos I don't believe in wars and all that kind of macho stuff. Boxing. Fighting. Beating people up. It's just sometimes, with Craig, I can see how it happens.

"You know," said Mum, "that was quite uncalled-for. It was also very unkind. Frizz is an extremely sweet-natured girl."

Craig said, "Yeah, but you wouldn't wanna go out with her." And then, obviously realising he had gone too far, he mumbled, "Not very pretty. Know what I mean?"

"Looks aren't everything," said Mum.

I said, "No, they're not, you squat-faced toad! Didn't notice Darcie seducing *you.*"

Craig's face darkened. "You don't know what went on between me and Darcie."

"Nothing, I shouldn't think," I said. "You only went out with her for about two minutes before she junked you."

"She didn't junk me, you blithering idiot! I junked *her.*"

"Oh, yeah?"

"Yeah!"

"Stop it," said Mum. "Stop it, stop it, stop it! Apologise to each other immediately!"

I sniffed. Craig scowled. As ungraciously as we could, we both muttered that we were sorry. Perhaps we really were; just a little bit.

"That's better," said Mum. "Now! Craig. What about

it? Surely it wouldn't do you any harm to go out with Frizz for just one day? I'm sure she's feeling terribly hurt and unsure of herself, and it would be a kind gesture."

Craig shuffled, uncomfortably. "See, there's Sam," he said.

"I seem to recall you were quite prepared to give Sam the elbow when you thought you were going with Lily!"

"Yeah, but that was Lily."

"Oh, look, forget it," I said. "I'll find someone else. There are plenty of other boys. *Nicer* boys. I'll ask Rees. He'll know someone."

"Wanna bet?" said Craig.

Mum picked up a handful of weeds and threw them at him. "You," she said, "are going through a very tiresome phase."

"It's the way I've been brought up," said Craig. He dodged another handful of weeds. "I blame the parents!"

With that, to my relief, he disappeared indoors.

"Frizz is too good for him, anyhow," I said.

Mum didn't make any comment; just went on with her weeding.

"Dunno what this Sam person's like…gotta be loopy, I should think, going out with him."

"I just hope she's nicer than Darcie," said Mum.

"I thought you said not to blame the woman?"

"Not *just* the woman; it has to be a bit of both. She certainly doesn't sound a very pleasant sort of girl."

57

"She isn't – she's horrible. I hate her! So does Frizz. And now she hates Darren, as well! Why do men *do* these things?"

"I suppose… " Mum sat back, considering. "I suppose, in a way, Darren felt flattered, maybe? He's not exactly Justin Timberlake, or whoever your current heartthrob is—"

I giggled. *Heartthrob?* Mum was so out of touch!

"Well, whatever," said Mum. "You know what I mean… To have a girl like Darcie throw herself at him…I'm not excusing his behaviour, but you can see how it happens."

"No," I said, "I can't! If Frizz wouldn't do it, why should he?"

Mum sighed. "Just a moment of temptation…it can happen to any of us."

"*Mum.*" I stared. "Has it ever happened to you?"

"Oh, when I was younger…a lot younger! Before I met your dad."

"But not since?" I looked at her sternly.

She laughed. "It's all right, you can relax! Your dad's the only man for me."

Phew! That was a relief. "I'm going up the park now," I said. "I'm going to meet Rees and walk the dogs. I'm going to ask him if he knows anyone who'd like to go out with Frizz."

"Yes, well, OK," said Mum, "give it a go. But,

Polly...don't push it! Don't fix her up with just anyone. You don't want her to get hurt all over again."

"God, she was willing to go with *Craig*," I said. "You couldn't get much worse than that!"

Rees was waiting for me at the park gates. Rufus and Bundle greeted each other like long-lost friends, wagging and wriggling and making whimpery noises, before tearing off together across the grass. Me and Rees did the human equivalent. We grinned (which is like wagging), and made as if to kiss but then didn't quite manage it (wriggling) and finally said, "Hi!" (whimpery noises).

It was always just a tidge embarrassing when we met up after a break (a week, in this case). I think we both felt that we *ought* to kiss, cos after all we were an item, but when it came to it, we were both too shy. It's pathetic, I know. I would never have confessed it to Keri. Maybe not even Frizz. I might to Lily, cos I was pretty sure she had never properly kissed a boy, either. Not with the tongue, and all. Even telling Lily, though, would have brought me out in a rash. It is so *very* shaming.

Rees and I set off after the dogs. We did at least hold hands; we had got that far. I liked the touch of Rees's hand clasped over mine, though I did sometimes wonder if perhaps I ought to feel a bit more...tingly? I'd once read a letter in a magazine where this girl said that every time her boyfriend touched her she felt "liquid electricity" shooting through her body, and wondered if this was normal. (Apparently it was.) She was only ten years old. I was twelve, going on thirteen, and I hadn't ever felt liquid electricity! I wasn't even sure what liquid electricity was. How could electricity be liquid? But I'd read somewhere else about tinglyness, which I guessed was probably like a sort of pins and needles, and I kept waiting for it to happen, but it never did. I would have liked to ask Rees if he ever felt it, only Rees and I didn't really discuss that sort of thing. Feelings and suchlike. I was scared it might embarrass him. I knew it would embarrass me!

I did like being with him, though, so maybe the tingly thing would come later. I made up my mind not to worry about it. Sometimes (if you're like me) you can worry so much that you simply never have any fun at all.

Rees swung my hand as we walked. "So, what've you been up to?" he said.

"Nothing much. What about you?"

"Well…" The words came bursting out of him. "There's this new manoeuvre I've discovered!" He sounded really excited about it. "I found it on the internet. Not many people know about it. It's brilliant!"

I guessed he was talking about chess. Chess is his big passion. He'd once tried to teach me, but I was such a dismal failure he'd had to give up. But he was obviously bursting to tell me all about it, so I assumed an alert, listening expression and did my best to make intelligent comments, such as "Ooh!" and "Wow!" and "Really?" at appropriate places. All I can say is I'm obviously not a very good actor. Rees wasn't fooled.

"Sorry," he said. "I'm boring you!"

I assured him that he wasn't.

"I am, I'm hogging the conversation. We're not even having a conversation! It's just me, droning on."

"You're not droning! You're being enthusiastic."

"I'm being boring! I know I have a tendency that way."

I giggled when he said that; I couldn't help it.

Rees grinned. "Mum says if I'm not careful I'll turn into a right regular blimp."

"My mum says if I'm not careful I'll turn into a worryguts!"

"*Do* you worry?" said Rees. He sounded surprised. Had he really not noticed?

"I get anxious," I said. "I imagine things. And then I dwell on them. And that makes me worry like crazy!"

"But what have you got to worry about?"

"Nothing, really. Not like some people." And then I told him about Lily, which I'd been dying to do for the last five minutes. "Keri was right all along! Well, and so were you, I suppose...you said you thought he was probably gay."

"And you nearly bit my head off for it!"

"Well, it just seemed so *prejudiced*."

"I didn't say there was anything bad about it."

"There is for Lily!"

"Yeah...I guess it kind of knocks things on the head, far as she's concerned. Hey! You two!" He made a lunge at the dogs, who were annoying a runner. "Stop that!"

"Lily is devastated," I said, trying out a new word I'd just learnt. "Totally devastated."

"I'll totally devastate those dogs if they don't behave themselves," said Rees. "Maybe we should take them to obedience classes?"

Normally I would have thought this was a great idea. Me and Rees at obedience classes with Rufus and Bundle...it could be fun! But right now, I wanted to tell him my news.

"It's even worse for Frizz," I said.

"What is?" Rees was holding onto the dogs' collars as another runner came pounding past. "What's worse for Frizz?"

Eagerly, I launched into the story for the third time. I had it off by heart, almost word for word, by now.

"That Darcie," I said. "She's such a slag! Though you can't just blame the woman, of course. Darren let himself be tempted. He was probably a bit flattered. Cos, I mean, he's not exactly Justin Timberlake."

Rees was looking confused, like he couldn't understand how Justin Timberlake came into it.

"Darcie is *sexy*," I said. "Darren is – well!"

"Not sexy."

"Precisely," I agreed. *Precisely* was another word I had recently taken to using. It had a good ring to it. "Frizz says she doesn't want anything more to do with him."

Rees pulled a face. "Poor old Darren."

"Poor old *Darren*?" I practically shrieked. "How can you say poor old Darren? It's poor old Frizz, if anyone!"

"Poor old Frizz… Rufus! Bundle!" Rees made another lunge at the dogs.

"It's very hurtful," I said. "I just don't understand why boys behave this way."

"We can't help it – we're genetically programmed," said Rees. "It's an evolutionary thing."

What???

"I read about it, in this book. It's quite interesting, actually. It said—"

I didn't want to know what it said. I wanted to talk about Frizz and Lily! But it wasn't any use, and in the end I just gave up. Boys don't seem to enjoy chatting the way girls do. I knew what Craig would say, cos he'd said it before: *Boys don't gossip!*

Like gossiping was something to be ashamed of. Something mean and malicious. When I'd told Frizz about Lily, and then told Lily about Frizz, there wasn't anything malicious in it! When things happen to your friends, you want to talk about it. Not just the bad things; good things, too! Cos when bad things happen, you're sad for them;

and when good things happen, you're happy. So it's only natural you'd want to talk. Well, I would have thought so. But boys obviously aren't interested; either that, or it makes them uncomfortable. Even sensitive boys, like Rees. Cos Rees isn't at all macho; he's a pacifist, like me. I still couldn't get a good discussion going with him, though.

Right at the last minute, as we were walking back towards the exit, I said, "You don't know anyone who'd like to come to Hastings, do you? Instead of Darren?"

"What, you mean like…with Frizz?"

"Yes, cos she couldn't come on her own – it would be horrid for her. And we can't just leave her out. It wouldn't be fair." Plus, if neither Frizz *nor* Lily came, that would only leave me and Rees, and Keri and Damian, or Leo, or whatever his name was. We all had to go! We were the Gang of Four. "You must know *somebody*," I said.

"I'm thinking," said Rees. "There's Paul Taylor—"

"Who's he?"

"Boy in my class. He hasn't got anyone, I don't think."

"Is he OK?" I didn't want to fix Frizz up with some kind of Stone Age jerk.

"Yeah, Paul's OK. Only thing is…he's a bit of a boffin."

"That's all right," I said. "So are you."

"You think *I'm* a boffin? You haven't met Paul! He's, like, way off the scale… I'm not sure he and Frizz would get along."

I bristled immediately. Frizz is my oldest friend, and I am quick to jump on anything that seems like an insult. "You mean she's not clever enough?"

"I didn't say that," said Rees.

But it was what he'd meant. I felt resentment sizzling up inside me. It's true that Frizz isn't too good when it comes to exams and stuff, but she's funny and generous and sweet-natured. Surely that ought to count for something?

"I bet if she was *pretty*," I said, "it wouldn't matter that she wasn't clever."

Rees mumbled something that I couldn't quite catch.

"*What*?"

"I agree it isn't fair," said Rees. "It's just...the way things are."

"So what does the Great Brain look like? Some kind of romantic daydream?"

"Just ordinary," said Rees. And then he grinned, a bit sheepishly, and added, "Actually, he's rather overweight."

"And he thinks he can pick and choose?"

"I can ask him, if you like. I'm just not sure—"

"Oh, don't bother!" I snapped.

"I'm sorry," said Rees.

"Why? What's to be sorry for? Like you said, it's just the way things are."

"Doesn't make it right."

"Would you go out with Frizz?" I said.

He hesitated.

"You wouldn't, would you? Cos you're a brain snob! You don't think she's bright enough!"

"It's not that," said Rees.

"So what is it?"

I could see him desperately trying to think of something to say. He found it. "Would you go out with Darren?"

"Might do."

"Even though you've got nothing in common? Cos that's what it is," said Rees, "it's having things in common. You gotta have stuff you can talk about. Stuff you can do together. You can't just go out with someone cos you feel sorry for them."

I knew that he was right. It was what Mum had meant when she said, *Don't push it.* I heaved a sigh.

"Don't worry, it'll all work out," said Rees. "Things always do."

I said, "Things always do *not*! Everything's going pear-shaped."

"S'pose we took the dogs to obedience classes?"

Well, and suppose we did? So what? How was that going to make things any better?

"Mum's got a friend that runs them. I could easily arrange it."

"They wouldn't let them in," I said. "They're too old."

"They're not old!"

66

"They have to be *puppies.*"

"No, they don't! Stop being so negative. I'm going to ask Mum if I can arrange it."

"Can't stop you," I said, "if that's what you want to do."

"But if I set it up," said Rees, "you will come?"

I said that I would, cos he was really trying, in his own way, to be helpful and to cheer me up, and it would have been churlish (another nice word!) to say no. But I couldn't help feeling that everything was just falling to pieces.

Chapter 5

"D'you know a girl in Year 10 called Sam Matthewson?" I asked Chloe, as we met up at school the next morning.

"Never heard of her," said Chloe. "Why?"

"Craig's going out with her and I want to see what she looks like."

"You could try asking Katie. Her sister's in Year 10. She'd probably know."

I asked Katie at lunchtime. "I don't want to *talk* to her," I said.

"She just wants to look," said Chloe. She giggled. "She's spying on her brother."

"I'm not! I just want to know what she's like. Can you see her anywhere?"

"She's over there." Katie nodded towards a group of Year 10s. "The ginger one."

I thought, *Ugh! I hate people with ginger hair!*

That is *such* a politically incorrect thing to say. It's not even true! Keri is a ginger ninja, and I don't hate her. I guess I was just resentful on account of Craig preferring this Sam person to Frizz.

I glowered at her across the yard. She was small and thin, with bright red hair and freckles, and a pointy nose. Nothing in the least bit special. Quite plain, really. Craig obviously had lousy taste when it came to women. First that vile Darcie, now this pointy-nosed creature. Of course, he would really have liked to go out with Lily, but then *loads* of boys would like to go out with Lily. That was why I wasn't as worried about her as I was about Frizz. Once she had recovered from Joel, she'd be able to get any boy she wanted.

"So are they dating?" asked Katie. "Her and your brother?"

"They've just started. Probably won't last. What's she like?"

"She's OK. She came to my sister's birthday bash – she seemed quite nice. Why, anyway? Is your brother having problems with her?"

"No," I said. "I'm having problems with him! I asked him to do me a favour, just one small, tiny favour. I asked him if he'd come to Hastings with us and keep Frizz company, and he's being really mean about it."

I could tell that Katie was curious, and wondering how Frizz came into it, but fortunately at that moment the bell rang and I was saved from having to explain. I didn't mind

69

explaining to Chloe later, cos Chloe is, like, my *special* friend; but it wouldn't have felt right talking to Katie and Chantal about Frizz, behind her back.

Chloe listened, enthralled, as I plunged yet again into the story. Unlike Rees, she drank in every detail. She agreed with me that Darcie was unspeakable. "That girl is disgusting!" She agreed that there was no excuse for Darren's behaviour. "I'd tell him where to get off!" She even agreed that there were times when boys could be incredibly dumb. "They'll just chase anything!"

"According to Rees," I said, "they can't help it. They've been genetically programmed."

"Pah!" said Chloe.

"Mum says they're poor, weak, helpless creatures… I think she was being sarcastic. It made Craig really mad! Now," I said venomously, "I'm the one that's mad."

"Cos he won't go to Hastings with you?"

"He'd go with *Lily*. He just won't go with Frizz. It's not like I'm asking him to date her, or anything! Just go out with her this one time."

"So why won't he?"

"Cos he's totally disobliging!"

"Ooh, cool word," said Chloe.

Me and Chloe collect words like other people collect bits of china or stuffed animals. It's part of the reason we're such friends. I suppose, actually – thinking about what Rees had said – I have more in common with Chloe than I do with Frizz. But Frizz is my *oldest* friend, and I couldn't bear her being unhappy.

"If I can't find someone to go with her, she'll be left out. I don't suppose," I said hopefully, "you know anyone?"

Chloe shook her head. "Not really."

"What about that boy you were going to ask? One that lives down your road?"

"Danny. Thing is," said Chloe, "I don't actually properly know him. Only just, like, to say hello to."

"And you were going to ask him out?"

She grinned impishly. "I was gonna give it a go!"

"I wouldn't *ever* be bold enough to do that," I said.

"Nothing venture, nothing gain," said Chloe. "But I can't really ask him to go out with someone else, can I?"

Regretfully, I agreed that she couldn't. "If only we weren't at an all-girls' school. It'd make life so much easier!"

"I know, this is totally unnatural," agreed Chloe, waving her hand at a gaggle of Year 7s. "It's why you have to go and pick boys off the street...cos you don't *know* any."

"At least Lily gets to mix with them, even if they are all gay."

"*All* of them?"

"Well, some of them – including the one she's got this big thing about."

"No!" shrieked Chloe. "Don't tell me!"

But then, of course, I had to. I'd forgotten she didn't know. So many things had happened over the last few days, I had difficulty remembering who I'd told and who I hadn't.

"So Keri was right, after all?"

"Yes, it's maddening. She was big-headed enough to begin with."

"Well, I suppose she is a kind of expert. I mean—" Chloe stopped. "Hey, I just had an idea! She knows loads of boys...why not ask her?"

Doubtfully, I said, "I s'pose I could."

"Well, why not?"

It seemed the obvious solution. Why hadn't I already done it?

I knew why: because the sort of boys that Keri knew were not the sort that would look twice at my friend Frizz. They were all rich, and posh, and spoilt. But I said that I would give it a go. I had to find *someone*, or our lovely day would be ruined!

I waited till after tea before ringing Keri; I knew she wouldn't be free before then. They keep very odd hours at her school, like almost every minute of the day is crammed with hectic activity. I guess it's because they're boarders and have to be kept occupied. I wouldn't want to be a boarder! I know it's supposed to be fun, what with midnight feasts in the dorm, and everyone stuffing

72

themselves with sardines and chocolate cake, ,and drinking lemonade out of their tooth mugs and making themselves sick, but I would hate not being able to cuddle Bundle, or snuggle down in bed in my own bedroom with a book.

Keri loves it, but Keri is a very confident sort of person. She likes nothing better than to be part of a crowd, organising everyone. She also happens to be a mad sports fanatic, which I think must help. I am not at all a sports fanatic. I blame it on the fact that I have to wear glasses; though even when I finally get to have contact lenses, which Mum has *promised* me, I still can't imagine that I will take pleasure in charging up and down a muddy field, whacking at a ball with a bit of wood. All too often, in my experience, it's arms and legs that get whacked, rather than the ball. Keri says I'm a wimp. She's probably right.

She answered the phone on almost the first ring. "*Polly!*" she said. "Was I right or was I right?"

Cautiously, not giving anything away, I asked her what she meant.

"Well, I assume you're ringing about Lily?" she said.

"Has Lily rung you?"

"Of course she's rung me!"

"*When*?" I said.

"Yesterday afternoon. I was going to call you, but I got sidetracked."

I felt like saying, *She rang me on Saturday.*

"I take it you've heard?" said Keri.

"About Joel?"

"I warned her! She wouldn't listen."

"She's very upset."

"She'll get over it. She didn't sound too bad. Anyway, plenty more fish in the sea."

I said, "That's easy enough for you to say."

Keri laughed. "If you will go to a *nunnery*—" The Nunnery was her name for the High School.

"I didn't ask to be sent there! And I don't know how Lily's supposed to find anyone else, when according to you they're all gay."

"Not all of them," said Keri. She cackled. "Just about ninety per cent! Maybe *I'll* have to look out someone for her."

That reminded me of why I'd rung. "Did Lily tell you about Frizz?"

"No, what?"

"She didn't tell you?"

"We only had time to talk for about two minutes. I meant to call her later, but like I said, I got sidetracked." She giggled. "New guy down at the stables…really cute!"

I made a vague gurgling sound. I knew she probably wanted me to ask questions, but I didn't feel like indulging her just at that moment. She obviously sensed my lack of interest.

"OK!" she said. "So what's with Frizz?"

"She caught Darren kissing Darcie White in the kitchen at Melanie Philpotts' party."

"Whoa!" Keri whinnied excitedly, like a horse. "Way to go!"

"It was that Darcie. She deliberately set out to get him."

"What on earth for?" said Keri.

"I dunno. Just cos she's like that, I suppose."

"Can't keep her hands off other people's property."

"Frizz is devastated," I said.

"Yeah, I guess she would be." I noticed Keri didn't say that Frizz would get over it. *Or* that there were plenty more fish in the sea.

"They had a very special relationship," I said.

"Practically an old married couple."

"And now she doesn't want anything more to do with him!"

"Kind of like a divorce."

"Thing is," I said, "she hasn't got anyone to come to Hastings with. I've tried getting Craig to come, but he won't. Well, he would if he could come with Lily, but Lily doesn't want him, and he doesn't want Frizz, so I was wondering...I don't s'pose you know anyone? Just to keep her company. Cos it would be horrid if she had to be left out."

There was a pause.

"It's not like a proper date," I said. "And as a matter

of fact, we haven't actually *fixed* a date. You were going to let me know, so I could tell Rees."

Suddenly, abruptly, Keri said, "I'm not sure we'll be going, now."

"*Not going*? Why not?"

"Cos Frizz isn't the only one that doesn't have anyone to go with! Believe it or believe it not," said Keri, "I am without a boyfriend at this moment in time."

I was stunned. "What happened to Damian?"

"*Damian*?" She shrieked in outrage. "I gave him the elbow weeks ago!"

"Sorry," I said, "sorry! I can't keep up. *Leo*. I meant *Leo*."

"Yes. *Leo*. Well." She sniffed. "Leo's gone."

"Gone where?"

"He's seeing someone else, if you must know!"

"Oh." I wasn't used to Keri's boyfriends leaving her; it was always the other way round. "I expect you'll find someone else easily enough," I said.

"Sure. I'm not worried!" I could practically see her tossing her head. "I'm working on this guy at the stables…Bart. He's the cutest thing on two legs! Problem is, I can only get down there weekends. I'm scared somebody might pinch him while my back is turned!"

"Well, if you really fancy him," I said, "why not ask him if he'd like to come to Hastings with us?"

"Ask him out?" said Keri.

"I would!" Well, I wouldn't, of course; I'm way too

shy. But Chloe had been going to ask Danny. "You could always give it a go," I said.

From the silence, I could tell that she was mulling over the idea. "I'll work on it," she said.

"What about Frizz?"

"Give us a break! I can't do everything at once. In any case—"

I did *so* hope she wasn't going to say it.

"It's difficult, you know? She's not really the type."

I didn't ask her what she meant; I didn't want to fall out with her. In a small, tight voice I said, "So what are we going to do about Hastings?"

"Guess we'll just have to forget about it," said Keri. "Might be able to fix it up later. Maybe—"

"Hey! Keri!" a voice suddenly shrilled in the background.

Keri said, "Yeah, OK, I'm coming. Pol, I gotta go! Be in touch."

The phone fell silent. I sat for a while, staring at it. I felt as if a cold, damp hand had slithered its way down my throat and was clutching at my stomach. I knew it was totally immature of me to be so upset, I mean, it wasn't like some earth-shattering tragedy had occurred; but I had been looking forward to our outing for simply ages! I couldn't believe it had all fallen to pieces – *and no one but me seemed to care*.

I heard Mum's voice calling up the stairs. "Polly, I'm

off!" She was on late shifts at the nursing home where she works. Normally I'd have at least gone out onto the landing to say goodbye; but I just yelled, "OK!" and went on sitting.

A few minutes later my phone started warbling. I'd never noticed before how annoying it was. I'd chosen the ring tone specially cos I thought it was cool. But it wasn't cool; it was just *intensely irritating.* I felt like smashing the phone with a hammer. Instead, not having a hammer to hand, I picked it up and said, "Yes?"

It was Lily, calling to let me know that she'd spoken to Keri. I said, "She told me."

"Did she tell you about Leo?"

I said that she had.

"So it looks like our day out won't be happening?"

"Well, you wouldn't have been coming, anyway," I said.

I didn't feel like gossiping with Lily. I made the excuse that I had homework to do, and heaved myself downstairs in search of food. I needed to comfort eat! Dad was in the kitchen, finishing off his dinner.

"Hello," he said, "what's up with you? Someone thrown a bucket of cold sick over you?"

I said, "Huh!" and tugged at the fridge door.

"So long as they hadn't been eating curry," said Dad.

Why do men *always* have to make jokes about everything?

"Come here!" Dad pulled out a chair. "Come and sit down and tell me about it."

"Nothing to tell. Just that everything's fallen to pieces! And all because of *boys*." I slumped onto the chair. "Joel's gay and Darren's a rat and Keri's boyfriend's gone off with someone else and now we've had to cancel our day out to Hastings!"

"That's a pity," said Dad. "I've just been having a long conversation with Craig on that very subject."

"*Oh*?"

"I think you'll find he's had a change of heart."

"Bit too late for that," I said.

"Well, cheer up! There's bound to be a next time. I'm sure you can re-arrange it when people have got their love lives sorted."

"If they ever do."

I helped myself to a mouthful of apple crumble and wandered into the hall, chewing.

"Oh, there you are," said Craig. "I just wanted you to know, so long as it's not an official *date*, I don't mind coming."

"Coming where?"

"To Hastings! Keep Frizz company. I'd sooner go with Lily, but I'm willing to make an exception, just this once. For you. Cos you're my sister. And she's your friend. But it's only just this one time! I don't want you asking me to do it again, cos otherwise she'll start getting ideas."

I said, "She won't get ideas cos we're not going, so it's all right, you don't have to put yourself out."

"Oh. Well. OK! I just wanted you to know that I would have. I made the offer."

"It's very noble of you."

"Well, I think it is!"

"I'll ring Frizz and tell her."

"Yeah, you do that. But don't make it sound like I fancy her!" I pushed past him and rushed back up the stairs. He called after me, "What about Lily?" I didn't bother to answer. I flung myself on my bed and called Frizz. "How's things?" I said.

"OK," said Frizz. "Did you ask Craig?"

"Yes, I'd got it all set up. He was going to come, then I rang Keri, and guess what? Leo's dumped her!"

I waited for Frizz to say, *No???* Instead, in these really bitter tones, she said, "Boys are like that. It's what they do."

"Not to Keri!"

"Why not? Had to happen sooner or later. They're all the same."

"Yes, but...*Keri.*"

"She's no different from the rest of us," said Frizz.

I sighed; I obviously wasn't going to get anywhere. I'd started to recover myself a bit by now and wouldn't have minded a cosy chat, but Frizz was plainly not in the mood. I wailed at her that everything was falling to pieces. "Keri says we'll have to give up on our outing! I'm sure she could find another boy if she tried."

"Prob'ly find a whole soccer team," said Frizz.

Was she being sarcastic? I decided that she was. It wasn't like Frizz.

"It's so annoying," I said. "Just as I'd fixed it all up with Craig! He was quite happy with the idea."

"Don't worry," said Frizz. "It probably wouldn't have worked, anyway. I expect he was only doing it as a favour to you."

"Craig doesn't do me favours!"

"Well, I don't think he *fancies* me."

"Shouldn't think you fancy him!" I said.

"Don't fancy anyone right at this moment…I've kind of gone off boys. So it's just as well, really."

I was the only one who cared.

Chapter 6

"So when are you going to Hastings?" It was the next day, at break. I was perched on a low wall in the sunshine with Chloe, watching Katie and Chantal bat a tennis ball about. "Have you fixed a date yet?"

Glumly I said that we had had to postpone. "Keri's boyfriend's gone and dumped her."

"Never?" Chloe's eyes practically jumped out on stalks. "That's gotta be a first!"

"Frizz said it had to happen sooner or later. Frizz has got very bitter," I said. "She's gone off boys completely."

"It's enough to make one," said Chloe.

"*Anyway.*" I sighed; a deep, trembly sigh that almost unbalanced me. "What with one thing and another, Keri says we'd better just forget about it."

"But you were so looking forward to it!"

"Yes. Well. I guess it's not the end of the world." I was trying hard to be brave and make like I didn't really care, but I obviously wasn't very convincing.

Chloe sat for a bit, frowning and kicking her feet against the wall. Then she suddenly said, "Would you like to come with us?"

My heart leapt – and promptly fell again. "Wouldn't want to push in," I mumbled.

"You wouldn't be pushing in!"

"But you said they all knew each other…all the boys."

"Well, that's OK. You're one of us."

"What about Rees, though?"

"He'll be all right! He'll get on. Hey! You two!" Chloe slid off the wall and called across to Katie and Chantal. "Is it OK if Polly and Rees come with us on Saturday?"

"Sure," said Katie.

"Why not?" said Chantal.

"She was going to go to Hastings with all her friends from her old school, but there's been a bit of boy trouble."

"Ooh, what?" Katie bounced herself up on the wall. Chantal settled beside her. "Tell, tell! I'm all of agog!"

I giggled; I was starting to feel better already. "*Agog*," I said. "You're all *agog*."

"That's what I said! Don't keep us in suspense…what have they been up to?"

We spent the rest of break happily gossiping.

"Trouble with boys," I said, "they're just not the same as us."

"Hey, hey, big discovery!" Katie and Chantal whammed

their hands together in a high five and almost fell off the wall laughing.

"No, what I meant—"

"Why didn't anyone ever tell us?"

"What I *meant*—"

"She's only just woken up to it!" crowed Chloe.

"*All I meant was, they're like an alien species!*" I roared at the top of my voice. A gaggle of Year 7s, on their way past, turned to stare. "They're actually programmed differently." It was what Rees had said, and I was coming to the conclusion that he was right. "Their brains are different. That's what the trouble is."

Chantal gave a happy cackle. "Trouble is, you can't live without them!"

"Well, you *could*," I said. "I once read somewhere that way back in the mists of time all the women lived together and all the men were kept out. They were only allowed in when the women wanted to have babies." I blushed as I said this. It seemed so gross! I leaned forward and pretended to fiddle with my shoe-lace. "Apart from that," I said, "they led totally separate lives."

"'S all very well," said Chantal, "but who'd want to?"

"This is the problem," Katie nodded. "Life would be kind of empty."

"Just imagine if they weren't here," said Chloe. "We wouldn't have anything to talk about!"

The bell rang and we made our way back into school.

It had been a really good session. Ever since Chloe had told me about going off to Brighton with the others, I had been feeling excluded. Now I was back in the loop!

As soon as I got home that afternoon, I called Rees to let him know about the new arrangement. "We've had to cancel Hastings cos of Lily and Joel not coming, and now Keri. The boy she was going out with...she's not with him any more." I paused, waiting for Rees to make some kind of comment. Perhaps it hadn't sunk in. "He's dumped her, actually," I said. "He's dating someone else. So she doesn't have anyone. So...that's why we're having to cancel."

Rees said, "OK."

OK? Was that it? Boys are definitely weird! I guess you just have to accept it.

"Anyway," I said, "you know my friend at school? Chloe?" He'd met Chloe. "She's going to Brighton on Saturday with Katie and Chantal, my other two friends. We're all in the same class. They're really nice – you'd like them! And they're clever," I said. "Chloe's practically a genius when it comes to maths." That would impress him, for sure. Rees is a bit of a genius himself. "They asked me if we'd like to go with them...you and me. Cos obviously they're going with their boyfriends, which'd mean there'd be eight of us, same as it was going to be when we were going to Hastings, so I've said that we'd go, if that's OK with you. You don't have to if you don't want! It's just I thought it might be quite interesting, cos, I mean, *Brighton*…"

"My dad used to live in Brighton," said Rees.

"Really?"

"When he was a boy."

Gushingly I said, "I would *love* to live there!" I didn't mean to gush; I just wanted him to know that I really, really wanted to go on this trip.

"Beach is a bit pebbly," said Rees. "Wouldn't be very good for the dogs."

Alarmed, I said, "We wouldn't be taking the dogs!"

"No, I meant…if you lived there."

"Oh. I see. Yes! Well. What d'you think? Shall we go? Cos I've told them that we will, but if you'd rather not—"

"I don't mind," said Rees. "We can go if you like."

"Are you sure?" I squeaked at him ecstatically. "I just thought it would be fun."

"Your wish is my command," said Rees.

It kills me when he says stuff like that! We arranged to meet at the station at eight-thirty on Saturday morning, and I went racing jubilantly downstairs to tell Mum. I couldn't help feeling how lucky I was, having a boyfriend like Rees. Always so polite, and so considerate. He would never do anything to upset me, or embarrass me. I said very solemnly to Mum, "When I consider how *some* people's boyfriends behave, I know I have cause to be grateful."

Mum seemed to find this amusing, I'm not quite sure why, but she agreed that Rees was "One in a million…you hang onto him!"

"I intend to," I said.

She laughed at that. I still don't see what was funny about it.

On Saturday morning we all met up as planned and travelled down to Brighton together. Oh! It all started out so promisingly. There was me and Rees, and Chantal and Ben, and Chloe and Jonathan, and Katie on her own because her boyfriend, Tyler, was already down there.

"He's going to meet us," said Katie happily. "Then he'll show us round and take us places."

We'd all been to Brighton before, mostly with our parents, but we didn't mind Katie being a bit self-important.

"Can we go on the pier?" said Chantal. "The pier is my most favourite place in the whole wide world!"

The boys agreed: the pier was number one on the list.

"They got dodgems on the pier," said Ben. "And a whole room full of slot machines! Could spend all day there."

Chloe immediately protested. "I don't want to spend all day playing slot machines! I want to look round the shops."

Ben and Jonathan both groaned. "You can do that at home," said Ben.

"Not like you can in Brighton. It's wicked down the Lanes!"

Chantal said, "Yeah, I'd like to look around. I want to get a birthday present for my mum."

The two boys rolled their eyes. Ben said, "Girls!"

Katie at once said, "*Boys!*"

"What's wrong with getting my mum a birthday present?" said Chantal.

Ben said, "Nothing, if that's *all* you're getting."

"I can get other things, if I want!"

"This is what I mean…you'll be there half the day, picking stuff over."

"Then she'll want to try it on," said Jonathan. "Then she won't be able to make up her mind… *Shall I have this one, shall I have that one—*"

"Now she wants it, now she doesn't."

"It's a serious business," said Chantal. "You can't just buy the first thing you look at."

"Why not?"

"Cos it's not what shopping's about! Shopping's about *choosing.*"

"See, with boys," said Ben, "we know what we want. We don't hang about – we just go straight in and get it. And that's it! Finish."

"That's not *shopping,*" said Chloe. "That's just boring!"

"They can't help it," said Katie. "They lack imagination."

The bickering went on, back and forth. It was all

perfectly amiable; just a kind of flirting, really. I'd have liked to join in, but I wasn't quite brave enough. Ben and Jonathan seemed really nice, but I'd only just met them and until I get to know people I am sometimes a bit silly and shy. I was quite happy, though, sitting in the corner with Rees. We held hands all the way! Chloe teased me, but for once I wasn't embarrassed. I even quite enjoyed it.

Then we got to Brighton and met Tyler, and right away I didn't like him. I know you shouldn't judge people by their appearance, but there was just something about him…he reminded me of a lizard. Not that I have anything against lizards, some of which I think are quite charming. But lizards are lizards, and human beings are human beings. And anyway, Tyler didn't look like one of the charming sort. He looked sneaky and sly.

Katie was obviously crazy about him, and in a way I could understand it. He was quite small and neat, with limp black hair that flopped down over his eyes, so that he had to keep brushing it back. He was also very dark, in a romantic kind of way. I am sure most people would have said he was good-looking. It was just this sinister, lizardy thing I didn't like. Every now and again he would flick his tongue out over his lips. Ugh! Horrible. How could Katie bear to kiss him? But she did; long and ecstatically. And didn't even care that we were watching her!

"What have you got in the bag?" she said, when she

89

finally prised herself away. He was carrying this big black bag slung over one shoulder. It looked quite heavy. Tyler winked and said, "Something for later."

"Hope it's something nice," said Katie.

"Would I bring anything that wasn't?"

I thought yes, he probably would – though I couldn't imagine what.

Chantal, growing impatient, said, "Come on, guys! Let's head into town."

We spent all morning on the pier. We played the slot machines and went on some of the rides, including the dodgems, where Ben and Tyler did their best to ram each other and got ticked off. Rees won a bracelet for me, chucking balls at coconuts, and we all had tattoos done at the tattoo parlour. Not real ones, I hasten to add! Mum would go ballistic if I had a real one, though I think they probably wouldn't do them if you're under-age. These were just semi-permanent. But really pretty! I had a rose, cos that's my favourite flower. I got it done on my arm, so I could show it off. Tyler seemed to think it was a bit pathetic and boasted that *he* had a proper tattoo – "But it's somewhere private!" I didn't know whether to believe him or not.

Chloe, who is quite bold, asked Katie if she had ever seen it; but Katie blushed and wouldn't say.

By the time we'd finished on the pier we were ready for something to eat, so we wandered along the front until we came to a booth selling food and drink. I bought a bag of crisps, a KitKat, a jam doughnut and a Coke. Oh, and I also bought a banana, as I thought that would be healthy.

We took the food down to the beach and crunched over the pebbles until we reached the water's edge. The sea was on its way in and was quite fierce, walloping about in great porpoise-like waves, so that every now and again the spray would break over us and we would shriek and move back. Well, some of us would shriek. Me and Chantal, mainly. After a bit Chantal said, "I've had enough of this! Let's go and look at the shops." She jumped up. "Who's coming?"

"You lot go," said Tyler. "We'll stay here."

"Why, what are you going to do?" said Katie.

"Oh, we'll find something, don't worry. But before you disappear—" He pulled his bag towards him. "Something to celebrate with...*da dum*!"

"What's that?" said Katie.

"What's it look like?"

"*Wine?*"

"Got it in one!"

"Where'd you get it?"

"Out the cellar." He grinned. "My dad's got about a thousand bottles down there. Here!" He'd even brought a corkscrew with him. He held out the bottle. "Pass it round!"

When it came to my turn I took only the tiniest sip, as

91

I really don't like the taste of wine. Specially red wine, which was what this was. It's all dry and sour. Well, that's how it seems to me. But I didn't want to be thought babyish, so I pretended I'd had a good swig.

"Does your dad know?" I said.

"Know what? Know I've helped myself to some of his best claret?" I felt my cheeks go red and wished I hadn't opened my mouth. Tyler look at me scornfully. "Course he doesn't! What do you think? It's all right, you can drink up – I've got another two bottles here."

"I don't want any more," I said.

"Suit yourself. Katie?"

I was quite relieved when Katie shook her head.

"Chloe?"

Rather primly, Chloe said, "No, thank you."

"Chant?"

Tyler thrust the bottle at Chantal, but impatiently she pushed it away. "I've had enough!"

"What's the matter with you?" jeered Tyler. "You're all a load of wusses!"

I was just so glad I wasn't the only one. We left the boys sitting there and scrunched our way back over the pebbles. I did hope Rees wouldn't feel I was deserting him, but I really wouldn't have wanted to stay there on my own, and I knew he wouldn't want to come shopping with us. Boys really don't understand shopping; it's something they just don't get.

Rees had once very sweetly offered to spend the afternoon going round the local shops with me. It hadn't worked. He kept asking me what I was looking for.

"What do you want to buy? You must have some idea!"

I had to explain that I didn't necessarily want to buy anything; I just wanted to look. I wanted to pick things up, and try things on, and plan what I'd wear if I were going to a wedding, or going to a party, or had a million pounds. He still didn't get it.

"You mean, it's like some kind of fantasy?"

I told him no, it was *practical.* "I'm preparing for when I *do* go to a wedding. Or a party."

Rees said, "What about the million pounds?"

I had to admit that that part probably *was* fantasy. "But anyone can dream!"

"Let's play a game," I said to the others, as we wandered about the Lanes. "Let's play, *if I had a million pounds...*"

"I wish!" said Chantal.

"Well, let's pretend," I said.

The things we bought!

"I can't carry all this," moaned Chloe, staggering under the weight of imaginary bags as we made our way back to the station to meet the boys.

Chantal twizzled imaginary earrings. "Emeralds," she

said. "I've always fancied emeralds."

"Suit you," said Katie.

"D'you think Ben'll approve?"

"Probably won't even notice!"

We'd arranged to meet at five o'clock, but at quarter past we were still waiting.

"Typical!" said Chloe.

"Maybe the tide came in and washed them away."

I wished Chantal hadn't said that! I was starting to worry, cos it wasn't like Rees to be late. And then we saw them, bowling into the station and stumbling towards us. Well, two of them were stumbling: Ben and Jonathan. They had their arms round each other's shoulders and were making strange honking noises, like geese.

"Omigod," said Katie. "They're drunk!"

Tyler didn't appear to be; and neither, to my immense relief, did Rees. They came to a halt in front of us. Ben and Jonathan stood there, swaying slightly, with foolish grins on their faces. At least they had stopped honking.

"I—" Tyler clapped a hand to his chest – "will see you—" he hiccuped – "to the train. If, that is—" he hiccuped again – "you have a train. Do you? Have a train?"

I looked at him with distaste. He was just as drunk as the other two. This was so gross!

"Let's go," I said to Rees.

We moved off, across the station. There was a bit of a problem getting Ben and Jonathan through the barrier as they'd started honking again, and flopping about on each other. Tyler tried to help, but only made matters worse by falling over. Rees, on the other hand, was being very quiet. I was so proud of him! *He* wasn't honking and hiccupping and falling over.

Katie hauled Tyler to his feet and told him to go home. Quite meekly, he obeyed. We watched him reel off again towards the exit.

"I s'pose he'll be all right?" said Chloe.

Katie shrugged. "It's not the first time."

I was really shocked by that.

"Lezzgerron," said Rees.

I said, "Pardon?"

"Gerron." He waved a hand at the train. "Siddown."

Katie giggled. "I think he wants to sit down!"

I turned to study him. He was looking quite pale. "Are you all right?" I said.

"Jusneedasiddown."

"Let's get them on the train," said Chantal.

"But Rees isn't well!" He looked as if he might be going to pass out. Wild thoughts rushed through my head. Dial 999, call an ambulance—

"It's just the wine," said Katie. "He'll be OK."

But he wasn't. No sooner had we got on the train and were sitting down than he put his head between his knees and was horribly, disgustingly sick. *And some of it splashed onto me.*

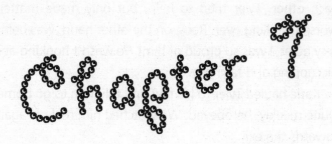

Chapter 7

"Mum, it was so embarrassing!" I wailed.

"I'm sure it must have been," said Mum.

"It went all over the floor! Some of it went on *me.*"

"Did you report it to anyone?"

I said, "Report it?"

"To get it cleaned up. All you had to say was that someone had been taken ill…you shouldn't just have left it."

Like it was me that was responsible!

"Oh, Polly," said Mum, "you didn't?"

Sullenly I muttered, "Katie cleaned it up."

"Really? That was good of her!"

"She had a towel," I said. She'd taken it with her in case we'd gone into the water. "Mum, there were *people* there. Watching! I just wanted to *die.* It's the most horrible thing that's ever happened to me!"

Rather briskly, Mum said, "I know it must have been

upsetting, but you did everything you could. It's not the end of the world."

"But he was drunk!"

"It happens," said Mum. "Try not to be too hard on him. He just did something silly." I looked at her doubtfully. "Now he's done it once, he probably won't ever do it again."

"Shouldn't ever have done it at all."

"Oh, Polly, don't be such a puritan! The poor boy must be feeling dreadful."

He must be feeling dreadful? What about me? My entire day had been ruined!

"You say there was this other boy—"

"*Tyler*. And two of his friends. We went off shopping and they just stayed there and drank! And it's not the first time," I added darkly. "Tyler's done it before."

"Then Tyler ought to know better. And don't tell me—" Mum held up a hand – "that so should Rees. I'm sure he's never done anything like this in his life."

"So why does he have to do it now?" The words came howling out of me. "He knew how much I was looking forward to today!"

"If the others were all drinking, he probably found it difficult to say no. It's peer pressure," said Mum. "You don't want to be the odd one out."

"But he puked over me!"

"A tiny little splash. Oh, come on, now! Put yourself in

his shoes…think how embarrassing it must have been for him."

"What about *me*?"

"Yes, and for you! I've already agreed. But you're not the one who's going to wake up tomorrow covered in shame."

"Better than being covered in puke."

"Oh, you are such a drama queen! The poor boy makes one little mistake—"

I shrieked, "*Little*?"

"There are far worse things he could do," said Mum.

I didn't ask her what; I didn't want to know. He'd shown me up in front of other people. Puking all over the place! It was *disgusting*.

"Give him a break," begged Mum. "I'm sure he's suffering quite enough without you rubbing it in."

"That's right!" I shouted. "Take his side!"

I turned and went crashing noisily out of the room. How could Mum possibly stick up for him? I wished I'd never told her! I should have told Dad. I bet *he* wouldn't like the idea of his daughter being puked over.

"Poll," Mum called after me as I galloped up the stairs three at a time. "Boys will be boys," she said. "Nobody's perfect."

Huh! Like that was any comfort? I'd been shown up in public. It was the most shameful thing that had ever happened to me.

I tore off my T-shirt. My *new* T-shirt. *Soiled.* Ugh! I scrunched it up and hurled it into the wastepaper basket. I couldn't ever bear to wear it again! Although, perhaps…it did seem a shame to waste a perfectly good garment. If it went in the washing machine… But I would always know which one it was!

While I was dithering, my mobile started on its warbling. I looked, first; to check it wasn't Rees. I certainly didn't want to speak to *him*. But it wasn't Rees, it was Keri, all bright and breezy.

"Polleee! Guess what? Good news! I'm back with Damian!"

What did she want me to say? Three cheers? Congratulations? "I thought you got rid of him," I said.

"Yes, well, I've taken him back. I have made *rules*," said Keri, "and he has agreed to keep them."

"Bet he doesn't!"

"We shall see. *For the moment,* he's behaving himself. So what I thought, I thought we'd do our outing thingie next Saturday." She giggled. "While he's still behaving! Is that OK?"

"Not really," I said.

"What d'you mean, not really?"

"You're the only one that's got a boyfriend!"

"Why? What's happened to Rees?"

I gave her the story. How they'd just sat there, drinking, while we went round the shops. "By the time we met up

99

at the station, they couldn't hardly *walk* straight."

Keri said, "Been there, done that."

"You've got *drunk*?"

"Not me! But Alastair did."

Whoever Alastair was. One of her boyfriends, no doubt, from way back.

"Anyway, we managed to get them on the train," I said, "then Rees went and *puked.*"

"Yuck!"

"Some of it," I said, "went over *me.*"

"Double yuck!"

"Not to mention the *floor.* Katie had to mop it up with a beach towel."

"What a hoot!"

I held the telephone away from me and looked at it, outraged. She thought it was *funny*? "It was just, like, totally *disgusting*," I said.

"Yeah, I can imagine. So what's with not having a boyfriend any more?"

"After *that*?" I said.

"Oh, lighten up!" said Keri. "They do it all the time. You'll get over it. Listen, I gotta go. Get back to me about Saturday, OK? Oh, and ring the others, would you? Let them know."

I didn't feel like ringing the others. I trailed back downstairs to put my T-shirt in the washing machine. Craig yelled at me from the sitting room, where he and

Dad were glued to some sports thing on the television. "What's all this about Nickers puking?"

"Where did you hear that?" I said.

Craig looked smug. "Wouldn't you like to know?"

"Mum told you!"

"I didn't," said Mum, walking past on her way to the kitchen.

"So where did he hear it?"

"I have my spies," said Craig.

"You mean, you've been *gossiping*," I said.

Dad called out to me. "Poll! Here a minute." I went over, somewhat reluctantly. "I gather you're pretty upset – which I can understand. But don't condemn him for all time! Your mother's probably too loyal to have told you, but in the early days, before we were married, I once disgraced myself. True as I sit here!"

Craig leaned forward eagerly. "What happened?"

"I'm not going into the sordid details," said Dad. "I just wanted Polly to know that even the best of us can make fools of ourselves – and that your mum forgave me. That's all."

I said, "OK." But it wasn't OK! Whatever Dad had done, I bet he hadn't puked in a railway compartment. I stomped back upstairs. I was seriously beginning to wonder if boys were more trouble than they were worth. What with Joel not letting on that he was gay, so poor Lily nearly broke her heart, and Darren behaving like a total rat, and that creep Leo giving Keri the elbow, and now Rees – Rees of all people! How could he?

I sat holding my phone. I wasn't going to ring him! And he almost certainly wouldn't dare to ring me. What, after all, could he possibly say? I wouldn't want to ring anyone after I'd puked all over them.

Maybe I would ring Frizz; she would be sympathetic. I tried her number, but it was engaged. I tried it again a few minutes later, and then again after another few minutes, and then again. Still engaged. Who could she be speaking to? In desperation, I rang Lily.

"Hi, Polly!" She sang it out, happily, down the telephone. "I just heard from Keri."

"I thought she wanted me to ring you," I said. I felt aggrieved, though I didn't really know why.

"Whatever!" Lily dismissed it airily. "She says we're all going down to Hastings next Saturday! I've already told Joel! He's OK with it, he's—"

"You're going with *Joel*?" I said.

"Why shouldn't I?" She sounded, for Lily, quite aggressive. "Just because he's gay doesn't mean we're not still friends."

I thought, *people are so odd*. I didn't remind her that last time we'd spoken she'd said if she couldn't come with Joel, she didn't want to come at all.

"What about Frizz?" she asked. "Have you spoken to her?"

"Not yet. But anyway, I'm not going to be coming."

Lily squeaked, "Polly! Why not?"

"Because Rees got drunk and puked over me," I said.

Of course she wanted the whole story.

"So that's it," I said. "I shan't be coming."

"Just because he got drunk?"

"And puked over me."

"Well, I know it can't have been very nice," said Lily.
But…?

"But, I mean…he did save your life that time!"

"Only rang 999," I muttered. "Anyone could have done that."

The line went silent and disapproving.

"What would you do," I said, "if Joel got drunk and puked all over the place? *In public?*"

"I expect I'd be a bit embarrassed," said Lily, "but mainly I'd think how he'd be feeling…cos if it was embarrassing for me, it'd be a whole lot worse for him. So I'd probably tell him it was all right, it didn't matter, it could happen to anyone."

"I beg your pardon," I said, rather coldly, "it most certainly could not!"

"Well, maybe not to you," agreed Lily, "but you're such a goody-goody."

Oh! Nobody had ever been that nasty to me before. "I'm not a goody-goody," I said. "I've got two order marks already this term! But one thing I am never going to do is get drunk. *Or* smoke. *Or* do drugs. *Ever.*"

"That's what you say," said Lily.

"That's what I know! I'm going to ring Frizz, now."

"OK. Hope you change your mind about Saturday."

I made a *hrumphing* noise and rang off. I was feeling quite disgruntled. What was the matter with everybody? First Mum, making excuses; then Keri saying "what a hoot"; and now Lily telling me I was a goody-goody! I dialled Frizz's number and *still* she was engaged. That disgruntled me even more. Just when I needed her! Cos I felt sure that Frizz, at least, would be sympathetic. She was my best friend: she would understand.

I wondered whether to risk ringing Chloe. I wasn't sure that I wanted to; she had been a bit giggly on the train. I was still trying to make up my mind when the phone rang of its own accord. It was Frizz, getting back to me. I waded straight in.

"Keri rang," I said. "She's back with Damian and she wants us all to go to Hastings next Saturday. You can go with Craig if you want, but—"

Excitedly, Frizz interrupted me. "It's all right! Me and Darren are together again."

I shrieked, "*What?*"

"We're back together." I could almost see her glowing pinkly down the phone.

"After what he did to you?"

"He was just, like, *so sorry,*" pleaded Frizz. "I had to

104

forgive him! He's promised it'll never happen again. We've had this long talk, and—"

"Was that him you've just been speaking to?"

"Yes." Now she was beaming; I could hear it in her voice. "He's apologised and I've forgiven him. So it's OK for Saturday! But what about Lily?"

I snapped, "Never mind Lily, what about me? Lily's all right, she's going with Joel. *I'm* the one that's not going!"

I told the story all over again. I reached the part where I got puked over. I waited for Frizz to screech. To cry, *Oh, poor you!* Instead, to my indignation, she cried, "Oh, poor Rees!"

Poor Rees? Had she taken leave of her senses? I was the one that had got puked over!

"He must have felt awful," said Frizz.

"What d'you think I felt?"

"Sorry for him?"

I couldn't believe it. I just *could not* believe it. Someone gets drunk and pukes all over the place and everyone feels sorry for them!

"I think you must be mad," I said, crossly.

"I can see it must have been horrid for you," said Frizz, "but honestly it's nowhere near as bad as what Darren did. If I could choose, I'd far sooner he got a bit drunk than kissed another girl. It's just that if you love someone—" She stopped. "I suppose if you *don't* love them...I suppose then it might be a bit different. Has he rung you?"

"Shouldn't think he'd dare!"

"No, it would take a lot of courage," agreed Frizz. "I don't know whether I'd be brave enough. I expect I'd probably just send a text...be easier that way."

"Not sure I'd answer even if he did."

"That would be unkind," said Frizz. She said it rather sternly, in this school-mistressy tone she sometimes uses. "I think you should call him."

I told her there would be no point. "I have absolutely nothing to say." I switched off the phone and went downstairs to join the rest of the family.

"Feeling any better?" said Mum.

I grunted.

"She bears grudges," said Craig. "She—"

"Craig, button it!" said Mum. "I thought you were on your way out?"

It was quiet after he had gone. I cuddled Bundle for a bit, and tried to concentrate on the television, but Dad was still watching sport and in any case I couldn't settle.

"Going back upstairs," I said to Mum. "Going to do some homework."

I did have homework, but I didn't feel like doing it. I picked up my phone, wondering whether to ring or not to ring. What would I say if I did? My thumb hovered and quivered. And then I discovered that I had a missed call, so I listened to the message and it was Rees. He didn't sound drunk any more; he sounded embarrassed. And ashamed. And apologetic. He said, "Polly, this is Rees. I don't suppose you'll feel like speaking to me ever again, but I just wanted to say that I am very sorry for what happened. I won't ring back in case you'd rather I didn't, but I'm just really, really sorry."

My heart kind of melted when I heard his voice. I didn't exactly *forgive* him, but...well. I thought it was brave of him to ring. So I called him back, and he said again that he was sorry, and I found myself saying that that was OK, it could have happened to anyone; and before I knew it I was telling him about Hastings.

"Keri's back with Damian, and Lily's coming with Joel, and Frizz says she still loves Darren in spite of him kissing another girl, so it's all on again! And this time there won't be any horrible boys with bottles of wine."

"Even if there were," said Rees earnestly, "I wouldn't drink any. I didn't even like it!"

"Me neither," I said. "I don't get what people see in it."

"Specially when they've had too much... I hope I didn't ruin your clothes."

"'S all right," I said. "It was only the T-shirt. I've put it in the machine."

"I really am very sorry."

I was glad that he had apologised, but I didn't like him

being humble. I reminded him that he had once saved my life.

"In any case," I added, "you know what they say...boys will be boys. Nobody's perfect!"

About the Author

Jean Ure had her first book published while she was still at school and immediately went rushing out into the world declaring that she was AN AUTHOR. But it was another few years before she had her second book published, and during that time she had to work at lots of different jobs to earn money. In the end she went to drama school to train as an actress. While she was there she met her husband and wrote another book. She has now written more than eighty books! She lives in Croydon with her husband and their family of seven rescued dogs and four rescued cats.

More Orchard Red Apples

❑ Pink Knickers Aren't Cool!	*Jean Ure*	978 1 84616 961 8
❑ Girls Stick Together!	*Jean Ure*	978 1 84616 963 2
❑ Girls Are Groovy!	*Jean Ure*	978 1 84616 962 5
❑ Boys Are OK!	*Jean Ure*	978 1 84616 964 9
❑ Do Not Read This Book	*Pat Moon*	978 1 84121 435 1
❑ Do Not Read Any Further	*Pat Moon*	978 1 84121 456 6
❑ Do Not Read Or Else!	*Pat Moon*	978 1 84616 082 0
❑ The Shooting Star	*Rose Impey*	978 1 84362 560 5
❑ My Scary Fairy Godmother	*Rose Impey*	978 1 84362 683 1
❑ Hothouse Flower	*Rose Impey*	978 1 84616 215 2
❑ Introducing Scarlett Lee	*Rose Impey*	978 1 84616 706 5 *
❑ The Truth About Josie Green	*Belinda Hollyer*	978 1 84362 885 9
❑ Secrets, Lies & My Sister Kate	*Belinda Hollyer*	978 1 84616 690 7 *